CHRIS KENISTON

Indie House Publishing

Indie House Publishing

BOOKS BY CHRIS KENISTON

Hart Land
Heather
Lily
Violet
Iris
Hyacinth
Rose
Calytrix

Farraday Country
Adam
Brooks
Connor
Declan
Ethan
Finn
Grace
Hannah
Ian
Jamison
Keeping Eileen

Aloha Series Heartwarming Edition
Aloha Texas
Almost Paradise
Mai Tai Marriage
Dive Into You
Look of Love
Love by Design
Love Walks In
Flirting with Paradise

Surf's Up Flirts
(Aloha Series Companions)
Shall We Dance
Love on Tap
Head Over Heels
Perfect Match
Just One Kiss
It Had to Be You

**Other Books
By Chris Keniston**

Honeymoon Series
Honeymoon for One
Honeymoon for Three

Family Secrets Novels
Champagne Sisterhood
The Homecoming
Hope's Corner

Original Aloha Series
Waikiki Wedding

ACKNOWLEDGEMENTS

I'll admit, *Rose* was tough to write. Not just because like Rose—I don't know fish—lol, but because in the middle of writing her story, my grandson was born. Well, apparently grandbabies trump book writing. I am blessed to have spent seven weeks helping my daughter adjust (that was the excuse hee hee) and enjoying my little bundle.

Once I got home, with the help of authors Kathy Sullivan, Barb Han, and Dale Mayer, I was finally able to finish Rose's story. You ladies are the best!

I'd be remiss if I didn't mention a longtime friend Randy Testutt for allowing me to interrupt his day and uncover my hero's career. Thanks Randy!

As much as I love my Aunt Mary's baking, and thank her for the first four recipes in the Hart Land series, for Rose I needed help. For giving us the delicious almond crescent cookie recipe I have to profusely thank my longtime fan Mona Kekstadt! Thank you ever so much for saving my day and increasing my waistline!

I hope everyone enjoys *Rose*!

CHAPTER ONE

"Watch your step." The voice attached to the tool-clad man in a yellow hard hat carried loudly across the small workspace. The man hadn't even bothered to look up, but staring at Rose Preston's feet, he shook his head. Only a construction worker could view a two-inch wedge heel with the same disdain as that of a five-inch stiletto.

"Thanks," she responded calmly. What she actually wanted to say was *I'll match my careful steps in heels to your steel-toed stomps any day.* Walking through a construction site had nothing on running through the woods at night in flip-flops with only the moon to guide her path. For a fraction of a minute she allowed herself the luxury of letting her mind drift back to the youthful days of lakeside summers. The next moment, she glanced at her wrist and sighed. If all went well she'd be on her way to Hart Land in little more than an hour.

Not truly a vacation, but even working at the lake was a joy. The distasteful image of a string of fresh-caught fish flashed in her mind. *At least she hoped so.* Tablet in hand and satisfied with the small exhibit's progress, she proceeded directly to the conference room.

Halfway down the main hall, Sarah, the best right-hand-man a woman could ask for, clutched a color-coded binder to her chest and fell into step beside her. "Jim texted that he's caught in the back up from a six car pile-up on I-93. I told him not to worry, we got this."

Without breaking pace, Rose cast a sideways glance in Sarah's direction. She'd feel much better about that comment if she wasn't about to spend the next two weeks dealing with… fishermen.

Sarah reached the double doors first and shoved them open, stepping aside for Rose to pass and take a seat at the massive table already buried in stacks of files and photos. "Did you get the condition report?"

"I did. Looks good." She nodded, studying the photos spread out on the table and running the new layout in her mind. They had a lot of work to do and she'd only had one cup of coffee this morning. Stretching her neck from left to right, she spotted the brewing pot of caffeine and headed over. "All the works look to be here."

"Yes. I did a walk through yesterday and confirmed." Sarah ruffled through papers in the binder, slid one out, and placed it on the table. They both used technology and electronics, but like Rose, Sarah was a tactile person and if heaven forbid the cyber world ever crashed, she and Sarah would still have everything they needed at their fingertips.

Feeling reassured at that silly idea, Rose turned back and set a mug down in front of Sarah, then holding the paper in one hand, returned to the coffee station. "This may be the first time customs hasn't found at least one thing to give me indigestion." Turning back, she set the sugar in front of her assistant curator.

"Thanks." Sarah tore the packet open and poured it into her mug. By the time she'd stirred it in, Rose had set the creamer beside her as well.

The photo captions for the exhibit publications were the next item to be handled. "It will be up to you to follow up with the printers. I'll have some access to internet—"

"I'll stay on top of it." Sarah took a sip of her coffee.

The only reason the thought of leaving for two weeks before a new, albeit small exhibit didn't give Rose apoplexy rested solely on how seamlessly Sarah kept pace with her. From the photo decisions, they pored over public inquiries, moved on to copyrights for the music, then scents for a visceral experience only to have the idea nixed for multiple reasons.

When the phone pinged from the conservator at the loan museum, Sarah took the call and once again the ease with which she handled the conversation gave Rose one less thing to toil over. All would be well.

A brief interruption ensued over exhibit supports with the designer and by the time lunch rolled around, they'd discussed marketing materials, the media preview, and personally checked the exhibit storage area. Her stomach growled and she knew another cup of java was not what her body needed.

The landline rang and Sarah was first to reach the phone.

"Good morning, sir." Her face brightened. "Yes, sir. Good to hear your voice too."

Rose didn't have to hear anything more to know who was on the other end of the line. Wondering why her grandfather hadn't tried her cell, she glanced down at her phone and saw two missed calls. She'd placed it on silent no vibrate in order to get through this morning's agenda quickly. The exhibit designer was marching in her direction carrying two different sized white panels. Sucking in a deep sigh, she mouthed to Sarah 'Tell him I'll call back when I'm on the road' and turned to deal with how major an impact would shifting from four foot to six foot display boards affect the original design. Suddenly any amount of time with fish and fishermen was looking really good to her.

• • • •

Straightening, Logan Buchanan stretched his shoulders and rolled his head left then right. It had been ages since he'd ridden a fence line with the crew and even longer since he'd done repairs. Rising before the sun and saddling a horse had been the easy part of this day. Once upon a time, he'd spent more hours on horseback than at the keyboard. For as long as he could remember, working beside his dad was as routine for him and his siblings as Saturday morning cartoons for the rest of the world.

"I don't know about you, but I'm ready for a snack." For Cal, snack was cowboy code for *could eat a cow*.

"Thinking the same." It had been hours since the big breakfast Maggie had made for everyone, and his stomach was beginning to protest.

"Didn't think we'd get that much work done." Cal slipped his gloves off and tucked them into his back pocket. He might be one of the youngest hands on the ranch, but he had the diplomacy of someone older and wiser. He could have just come out and said he'd expected working with a desk jockey like Logan to slow them down.

Logan chuckled. "I guess it's like riding a bike. Some things you don't forget."

"Guess so." The kid checked his phone, slid it into his other pocket and then reached into his saddle bag for a bottle of water, his gaze scanning the distance for signs of lunch.

Logan didn't blame him. They'd put in a hard morning's work and he might easily *snack* on a side of beef himself.

"How you holding up?" Cal asked. "I mean, real work can be hard on a guy."

So much for youthful diplomacy. After all, he wasn't *that* old. Except for a little stiffness in muscles that hadn't been used since the last time he'd chipped in to work the cattle or the fences, it felt good to get away from the office and away from his computer. Not that he didn't love all things electronic, but Texas fresh air and working the land was in his blood as much as the telecom corridor. If he had to choose between the two, it would be like asking which leg would he cut off.

The two ranch hands who had worked the fence line on the other side of the north pasture rode up in a four-wheeler. He wasn't sure who was younger, the two hands or his favorite boots. No wonder Cal was treating him like an old man.

"Hank called. He's bringing lunch."

In the distance, the dust kicked up. The ranch Suburban came to a stop and Hank, the senior foreman who had been with the ranch since Logan was tall enough to mount his own horse, climbed out and walked over. His gait was that of a man who had spent more time on a horse than behind the wheel of a motor vehicle. "Maggie made her peach cobbler for dessert."

Whistles, hoots, and wide grins broke out. Logan had to admit, the woman made a mean cobbler. The hatch open and the tailgate down, the back of the Suburban hosted a buffet spread fit for a king, or a hardworking cowboy.

"I hear you're heading up north?" Hank asked, filling up his own plate.

"Yeah. Gramps and I are going to help out a buddy of his throwing his first fishing tournament."

Hank shook his head. "I can understand an afternoon at the creek, but I want to eat my catch not weigh it."

Funny how he'd felt the same way until he'd done his first tourney with his grandfather.

"Boy, what are you doing?" Hank frowned at Cal.

A biscuit in one hand, chomping away, the kid was playing a game on his phone with his other hand. "Bait and Fish."

Hank's brow rose high on his forehead. "What?"

"It's a game," one of the hands answered. "Everyone's playing it. It's bigger than Angry Birds."

"Angry what?" This time Hank's brows buckled in confusion. Poor guy didn't stand a chance.

Suddenly Logan felt much younger. Though he had to admit, it wasn't often anyone found a cowhand using his lunch break to play games on his phone. At least the kid had good taste.

Hank's head snapped around to Logan. "And what are you grinning at?"

"Me?" He bit back a smile. "Nothing."

"God…" Cal started, frowning down at his phone.

"You'd better not be thinking of taking the lord's name in vain," Hank snapped.

"I can't get past level five. I've been at this forever. Keep falling out of the canoe."

"Let me see what you're doing." Logan leaned to one side for a better view of the kid's screen.

"You play?" Cal asked.

"Some." He shrugged. "Don't go so fast. That's the mistake everyone makes. This isn't speed, it's endurance. And don't waste your bait."

Cal frowned and shoving the last morsel of biscuit in his mouth, used two hands to tackle the game. Five minutes later the kid threw his arms into the air and sprang to his feet. "Level six, here I come!"

"Yeah, well." Hank pushed to his feet. "Level six will have to wait till after you finish working this fence line."

"Yes, sir." Without hesitation, Cal slid the phone into his pocket, placed his hat on his head, and just like that, the eager gamer gave way to a hard working cowboy.

There was something to be said for slowing down. His grandfather was probably right. A little time up north would be really good for him. A few hundred fishermen aside, just him, his gramps, and the fish. What more could a man ask for?

• • • •

Some days the idea of returning to horses for transportation held enormous appeal for Rose. Even if the beautiful animals couldn't travel at sixty miles an hour, a good horse could probably get her across Boston in less time than a fast car stuck in rush hour traffic. Which brought a whole other question to light. Why did they still call it rush *hour* when the business commute time had become more like rush *four-hours*. At times like Fridays and holiday weekends—or like today, when there was an accident—rush *half-a-day* was more appropriate. It had taken most of what should have been the almost three-hour drive to get to the lake just to escape the Boston area.

Now she'd turned off the main highway and onto the country roads that would take her to Hart Land. Already her blood pressure dipped and she could feel the tension that had taken residence in her shoulders easing away. So many shades of green hung over the drive; she loved Mother Nature's canopy. This was the way traveling should be. Not even a bumpy ride in a hundred year old carriage would have mucked it up—or the ringing of her cell phone. Hitting accept call on her steering wheel, she smiled at the General's name on her dashboard. "I'm almost there."

"And good afternoon to you too. The least you can do is wait for me to ask the question before answering."

"And why would I want to do that when I already know the question? Cutting to the chase saves time."

"Young lady, this is not Boston. Life on the mountain is not about saving time."

Wasn't that the truth. She sucked in a long deep breath of fresh mountain air. "Yes, sir."

"Now." She could hear his hands clap together enthusiastically.

No doubt he'd used his laptop to call her. Ever since his Annapolis reunion last year, the old guy had become practically addicted to his computer. Few things in life were as entertaining as catching him doing screen time with another old military man and reliving the antics of their college years. Tough old dogs.

"I know how hard it is for you to let go of control," the General said.

Pot calling the kettle black. "I like things in order. There's a difference."

"Yes, there is." She could hear his smile.

Of all the grandchildren, she was the most military in her thoroughness. If not for the need to rise before the sun and wear the most ghastly shades of khaki, she might have entertained a military career. Then again, there was no way she'd be the one doing the commanding at her age if she had.

"As I was saying," her grandfather continued, "I expect you to take it easy for at least a couple of days. Relax. Refresh your card playing skills."

She almost laughed at that one. There was no refreshing. She could annihilate the competition at cards since long before high school. That thoroughness allowed for an almost computer-like accounting of cards played. She didn't even need a color-coded system to keep track. "Don't you worry about my skill set."

"No. I suppose not." He chuckled. That sound was music to her ears. The gruff old man would always hide his tender heart behind his crusty Marine exterior. Whenever the shields came down was always extra special for any of his granddaughters. She was no exception. "I also thought it would be a good time for you to learn a bit more about—"

No, don't say it.

"Fishing."

He'd said it. At the ripe old age of six, she'd been bamboozled into doing "something fun" with her grandfather. Catching and handling slippery, slimy, wiggling, soon-to-be dead fish had not been fun. And she'd not been cajoled, coerced, or convinced to try it again since.

"We'll see." That response had worked about as well on her grandfather as it would on a six year old when her parents were actually saying not-likely-in-my-lifetime, but it was safer than outright digging her heels in the dirt.

"I bought you a fishing pole. It's pink."

"General," she bit back a laugh, "that hasn't been my favorite color since I was seven."

"Hm. Purple?"

"That's Poppy." Or maybe it was Callie. "Regardless, it doesn't matter if it's fourteen karat gold. I can run a successful art world fundraiser without learning to paint. I'm sure an auction at a fishing tournament will work the same way."

"We'll see."

Two words that made her cringe. When voiced by a retired US Marine Corps general, the words held a completely different meaning than when uttered by young parents. Already she was considering what outfit had she brought that would match a pink fishing pole.

CHAPTER TWO

This was not the first time Logan had been north of the Mason Dixon line, but he'd forgotten how peacefully green the northern scenery could be. Since leaving the freeway over an hour ago, the canopy of leafy trees that hung across the roads gave a startling contrast to his Texas ranch country. He loved the deep blue sky that covered the Texas landscape like a warm blanket, but he had to give credit where credit was due, the cool breeze blowing under nature's shady roadside arbor was considerably more pleasant than baking in hundred degree heat. Not that Texas didn't have summer breezes, they did—sometimes. Except, rather than refreshing, it was mostly a matter of moving hot air around.

According to the GPS, he would be arriving at the lake a lot sooner than expected. For the first time in ages, his flight actually arrived in Boston a half hour early. Next, his bag was surprisingly the first one out on the carousel. Then the shuttle bus to the rental agency had been parked outside the terminal as if waiting for only him, and not a single person stood in line in front of him at the counter. Even more surprisingly, he didn't hit any traffic at all leaving the city. If this was a sign of things to come he was about to break world records for fishing.

Since his grandfather's flight out of Houston was scheduled to depart shortly after Logan's arrival in Boston, they'd agreed for Logan to head on up to the lake and the General would send a car for his grandfather. Gramps' name on his cell phone surprised him. "Flight running late?"

His grandfather cleared his throat. "About that."

There was nothing about those two words that could precede anything good.

"Somehow your grandmother and I got our wires crossed."

He didn't like the sound of that for a multitude of reasons.

"She's doing her stress test day after tomorrow. You know how nervous she gets with anything doctor related. Even if it's only routine."

Logan nodded. No one was sure what had happened to his grandmother during her childhood that had left her so skittish about doctors, but for as long as he could remember, she'd done her best to avoid them.

"Your Aunt Margaret could take her but, well…"

"Yeah, I know." Logan held back a sigh. He couldn't fault the guy. Not only didn't the lady like doctors, but for too many years his grandmother had had to do things on her own while her husband was stationed on a ship or some other place unfriendly for wives and families. Gramps had been doing his best to make up for it ever since he retired.

"So you understand?"

"Of course. But it's a multi-day event. If you catch a flight afterward I'd be more than happy to stay on a couple of extra days." And he would. Quality time with his grandfather happened less and less, and at his age, who knew how much longer he'd be around.

"Sounds like a plan. I'll keep you posted. I'm counting on you to show the General and all the others how to reel 'em in."

Logan smothered a laugh. He doubted there was anything he could show his grandfather's longtime friend that he didn't already know. "I'd like it better if we could show him and everyone else together."

"I know, but you'll catch a real prize on your own. I can feel it in my bones."

Logan didn't know why, but he'd swear his grandfather wasn't talking about fish anymore. "I'll do my best."

"Of course you will."

As much as he loved fishing, it was time with his grandfather that he'd truly been looking forward to. By the time he'd pulled into the narrow drive toward the large white Victorian home on Hart Land, Logan had made up his mind that if his grandfather didn't join him for the tournament, then his next stop would not be home but to visit his grandparents. If he actually flew home, one thing or another would stop him from making the four hour drive. It always did.

A cool breeze brushed his face as he stepped out of the car. Maybe, even without his grandfather, this trip wouldn't be such a bad thing.

"Welcome," a soft voice called from over his shoulder. A lovely blonde in a pink t-shirt with her hair knotted in a loose bun bounced down the stairs. "Checking in or looking for someone?"

"Checking in." Most of the tournament fisherman would be staying at the larger nearby inns that dotted the lakeside landscape, but his grandfather had insisted they stay close to his friend. "The name is Buchanan. Logan."

"Nice to meet you. Callie Nelson." Smiling, she extended her arm. "My grandmother is inside. Do you need help with your bags?"

He shook his head, about to speak, when a slightly younger brunette in a flowing dress skipped down the steps and handed the blonde a whistle. "You forgot this."

"Thanks. Remind me again why I agreed to coach basketball camp?"

The brunette chuckled. "Because you love kids and you love sports and you're a sucker for anything that involves both."

"Oh, yeah. That's right." The blonde, Callie, beamed then briskly walked toward a parked car, waving her finger over her shoulder at Logan. "He's checking in."

"Great. Follow me." The brunette started up the stairs, twisting to talk as she walked. "Nice to have you. I'm Poppy. My grandmother is inside. She'll be happy to take care of you."

"Thank you." He couldn't help but shake his head, wondering if his grandfather had known about the plethora of attractive young granddaughters at Hart Land. What was Logan thinking—of course the old man did.

The minute he crossed the threshold, a graceful, attractive older woman with silver hair cut sharp above her shoulders glanced up and smiled. A sense of being home took over and any lingering resentment at not having his grandfather here slid away.

"You must be Mr. Buchanan."

"Yes." He didn't know if they had so few guests or if the woman was a mind reader or perhaps they simply kept that good track of what time each guest was scheduled to arrive.

"I understand your grandfather won't be joining us after all." She pulled a key from the drawer of a wonderfully preserved antique desk. "My husband will be sorry to hear that. He was looking forward to visiting."

"I'm hopeful he'll still join me, though a few days later than planned."

"Oh," her smile grew impossibly brighter, "that would be lovely."

For most people her pat responses would be considered polite platitudes, yet he was absolutely sure the woman was completely sincere. "Yes. It would."

She handed him the key. "Your cabin is across the way. You've been well stocked, and if you want to take advantage of your early arrival, I'd be happy to share some of my husband's favorite fishing spots for you to check out." She leaned forward, glancing left than right, and whispered, "Just don't tell him where you got the tip." She leaned back, chuckled softly and Logan decided this trip could prove to be the most fun he'd ever had at a tournament. For now, all he wanted was to sit back, relax, and enjoy the take-out dinner he'd picked up on the road. Tomorrow would be soon enough for a little reconnaissance.

• • • •

"What are you doing up so early?" Tying the apron behind her back, Lucy strolled into the kitchen in a direct path to the pantry.

"Thinking." Rose lifted her mug in Lucy's direction. "There's a full pot."

The family's lifelong housekeeper, well, at least as much of Rose's life as she could remember, glanced at the coffee machine in the corner. "I know you can brew a decent cup, so I won't fuss much at you over that, but whatever you're working on over there must be pretty important to have you up and thinking this early after playing cards with Ralph and the crowd until past my bedtime."

"Not really." She'd thought for sure staying up late combined with real fresh air would have had her sleeping like a teenager until at least mid-morning. Instead she'd risen with the proverbial chickens. Apparently her mind hadn't gotten the memo that she was on a sort of vacation. She also knew darn well that Sarah could handle the museum's to-do list with her eyes closed. Especially since this new temporary show was one of their smaller exhibitions, but that didn't mean Rose couldn't go over the details in her binder one more time, just in case.

"Well, isn't this providence?" With a tail wagging Golden retriever at either side of him, the General came through the doorway. Sarge and Lady immediately pranced up and plopping their wagging tails down on either side of her, each set their head on her lap.

Without a thought, she lifted a hand to pet each canine. Like a healing hand, she felt the tension bleed away.

The General made his way to the coffee pot. "The air smells just right for fishing."

"Since the tournament starts in a few days, that's probably a good thing." Lucy cracked some eggs into a mixing bowl.

The General took a sip of his coffee and turned to Rose. "Your grandmother suggested I give you the blue fishing pole to try instead of the pink one. I left it by the door if you want to look at it on your way to change."

"Grams, huh?" Rose mumbled, glancing down at the two dogs still resting their heads on her lap. Only lifting their gazes, the two looked up at her with huge brown eyes. She would almost be willing to swear an oath that she could hear them thinking, *You might as well give in.* Now all she had to do was find something to wear that didn't clash with a blue fishing pole.

The General clicked his heels and the two dogs hurried to his side. "Lucy, can you pack us a nice breakfast in a box?"

Lifting her brows in surprise, Lucy glanced at Rose and tipping her head slightly to one side, seemed to be waiting for a cartoon bubble to pop up overhead alerting her how to respond. Finally, she nodded. "How about some breakfast burritos? Easiest thing to eat on a bass boat. I'll send you off with a fresh thermos of regular coffee too." Her gaze shifted to Rose. "I think someone is going to need it today."

"Excellent. And throw in some of those almond cookies Lily dropped off." The General scratched the top of his dogs' heads. "I'll get the boat ready and meet you by the Point in fifteen."

Shaking her head, Lucy walked away mumbling something about a balanced meal.

Rose nodded and stood. Experience told her that fifteen minutes meant exactly that. Not fourteen and fifty seconds nor fifteen and ten seconds. With her mom updating the family cabin again, Rose was glad she'd decided to stay at the big house. At least she'd save five minutes walking down the hill and five more walking back.

The museum binder under one arm, she took the grand staircase two steps at a time and bolted down the hall and into her room. She'd had the good sense to unpack before dinner. Flinging the closet doors open, now all she had to decide was how to layer for a country morning with, heaven help her, fish. Clock ticking, she grabbed a pair of pressed jeans, a pastel blue button-down shirt and a lightweight jacket to match. Years of running late for school had taught her to braid her hair on the move. By the time she hit the ground floor running, she was dressed, her hair was out of her face, and the museum world safely tucked away in a dresser drawer.

"Thought you might need this." Lucy stood at the bottom step, extending an arm with a travel mug in hand.

God Bless that woman. A second cup of coffee was exactly what she needed.

"And remind your grandfather that a real lunch is precisely at noon today."

If fate was on her side, she wouldn't be gone anywhere near that late. "Will do."

Twenty minutes later they'd stopped at the General's favorite fishing spot at Morton's Cove. Except the last thing she wanted was to catch fish. At least not if she was expected to handle them. And there was no doubt that she would be, especially now that she wasn't six years old any more. She'd survived baiting the hook with live worms, but she wasn't capable of dealing with dying fish. Time with the General or not, she was done with the fishing and ready to go home.

"Let's try it again," the General said, standing behind her. "Control the distance by slowing the line with your thumb."

What she wanted to control had nothing to do with distance, unless it meant how far to reach for one of those almond cookies tucked away in the cooler. "Yes, sir."

Once again, for the umpteenth time this morning, she'd repeated casting the line. According to her grandfather, the process was a little bit science, a little bit art, and a lot of patience. Apparently she had none of the above. All she knew is that casting overhead looked a heckuva lot easier on TV. Giving it all she had, she managed to span the distance to the shore and snagged an inflatable raft from the nearby dock.

On a heavy sigh, her grandfather helped her reel the line back in. "I'll stop by Earl's place later today and bring a new float."

"Thanks." She should probably be the one making the peace offering since she was the one who'd hooked the water toy, but anything to distract her grandfather from dragging her back out onto the lake.

"Maybe we're going about this all wrong. Perhaps we should try a sidearm cast."

Just how many different ways were there to cast a line? Not that she was going to ask, the answer might take longer than her allotted time off from the museum. "We should probably get back to the house. There's so much still to coordinate. I promised Nadine I'd help confirm all the accommodations and the arrival of our welcome gifts."

"One last try," the General cajoled.

Rose knew there was no resisting that impish grin. She just hoped one last try didn't turn into two or seven. Bringing her rod back to her side and holding the button, she made her best effort at a circular swooping motion the way the General had shown her. Snapping her wrist forward and releasing the button, the line flew out. Who knew the thing could extend as far out as when she'd tried overhead. Flying toward the shore, the tiny worm lure and the flick of her wrist propelled the line past the dock, and up to the shore by a thicket of brush. The slight bit of resistance told her she'd snagged something else. And whatever she'd hit weighed more than the inflatable raft. "I seem to have caught something."

"Probably a tree limb. Happens all the time."

She made another effort to reel whatever she'd caught in.

"Careful. Pull too hard and you'll only break the line."

The line was the least of her problems. If her grandfather insisted on bringing her out until she mastered the art of casting, she might wind up at the lake until she was old enough to collect social security. Another tug and whatever she had seemed to break free. The reverse force knocked her back onto her butt.

"Are you all right?" Concern took over the General's expression.

"You know what they say, the only thing hurt is my pride."

"Fortunately," the General relieved her of the pole and spun to reel it in, "pride has a very brief recovery time."

She'd be more likely to agree over a hot cup of coffee and a few cookies. Or maybe a homemade donut.

"Oh, dear."

Rose glanced up. Something bright and yellow cut a wake across the water. Focusing really hard, not until the General had the item within arm's length did Rose realize her prize catch came in the form of one neon yellow vest. Squinting at the distance, she heaved in a deep breath. What the heck had she done?

CHAPTER THREE

B

y the time Logan realized the tug on his shoulder wasn't a wayward bird or steroidal insect, but a fishing hook pulling him toward the water, he'd already lost his balance. Scrambling to un-zip his vest, his feet pedaled like a duck underwater, all the time battling the determination of the person at the other end of the lure. One hard yank, and he slid into the water and out of his vest. Not the way he had planned his morning to go.

Heaven knew, he'd been caught, scratched, pinched, and hooked by neophyte fishermen on some of the best lakes in the country, but this was the first time anyone had actually succeeded in reeling him in. Well, at least reeling him off the shore and into the water. Sitting up to his waist in the chilled lake, he watched his favorite vest glide across the calm water before being snatched up by two people in a small boat.

Cold and unhappy, he pushed upright, keeping his eyes on the fishermen. Unable to make out their faces, he could see the two figures scanning the distance for the source of their latest catch. It was obvious the moment they connected the dots of the lone man standing in almost icy water and their latest catch. The heavier set of the two threw the garment to one side and waved for the redheaded silhouette to take a seat. By the time Logan had taken his shoes off and poured the water back into the lake, the boat was close enough for him to make out at least one of the faces. The General. This morning's conversation had consisted of a polite greeting and suggestions for the old man's favorite fishing spots. When they'd agreed to chat more later, he was pretty sure this had not been what either had in mind.

"Ahoy," the General called to him.

"General." What more could he say? He was wet, smelly, barefoot, and not at all prepared for a visit. He'd seen enough photos of his grandfather and his longtime friend to easily recognize the man when they'd met on Logan's way to his car, but he had no idea who the redhead was with the retired Marine. Though now that they were closer, he could see she was about the same age as the two granddaughters he'd met earlier. All of them natural beauties. Holding a bright blue fishing pole that matched the blue in her jacket, this granddaughter—if that's what she was—was no exception. For whatever reason, standing in icy water rather than attempting to get his footing on dry land, he stood frozen, unable to drag his gaze away from the deepest green eyes he'd ever seen.

"I am so very sorry." The redhead leaned so far over the boat as the General approached that for a split second Logan's heart lurched thinking she might fall in.

"I too must apologize, and accept full responsibility. My coaching skills on casting might be a bit rusty." Close enough to hand Logan his vest, the General extended his arm. "We need to get you back to the house to dry off. Why don't you climb in and we will come back for the car later."

Logan shook his head. "That won't be necessary. I can drive myself back."

"Won't you please reconsider?" The pained expression on the redhead's face took him by surprise. "If nothing else the car will end up sopping wet and you won't be able to go anywhere for at least a day, and most of that will be spent trying to get the smell of wet lake out of the car."

She had a point. On top of that, the shortest distance between two points was a straight line, and at this moment, the straightest line was across the water, not the winding country roads.

The General must've noticed his hesitation. "My granddaughter is right. Besides, my Fiona would be very unhappy with me if I left you to your own devices when it's our fault your morning plans are spoiled."

About to open his mouth and protest one last time, Logan recognized the glint in the old man's eyes and the tone of his voice. His words were not a suggestion, but an order. "Yes, sir. If you'll give me a moment to gather my things and lock the car we can be on our way."

"Of course." The General smiled, and motor low, steered the boat closer to shore.

In order for Logan to climb in without tipping the boat, the General and his granddaughter shifted to the opposite side until he was seated across from them.

"If it makes you feel any better," the redhead started, "I can assure you this will not happen again. I have put away my fishing gear," her gaze drifted momentarily to the General, "permanently."

Anybody else and he most likely would have come back with something along the lines of *not soon enough*, but the contrition in her voice and concern in her gaze wouldn't let him. "Please don't do that on my account. This isn't the first time I've gotten wet fishing." He shot her his best effort at a reassuring smile. "And I'm pretty sure it won't be the last."

"That's very kind of you, but I still have no business on the casting end of the rod."

That might certainly be true, but there was no way he was going to say that.

"Now, Rose," the General said softly.

Rose. The name suited her. What was that line about by any other name?

"Face it, General, the tournament simply cannot afford to have me out here learning to cast and alienating heaven knows how many more fishermen and guests. Trust me," her tone shifted to one of authority, very similar to moments ago when her grandfather had insisted he return to the house with them, "I do not need to know how to fish to do my job."

Her job?

"Of course not, it's just that—"

"General," she cut him off. "Trust me."

Logan had no idea why the General needed to trust her, but at this point, having known her only a few minutes and drenched from head to toe because of it, he was willing to trust her with anything she wanted.

When it appeared the debate was settled, Logan looked up and saw the old man had been right. The ride back across the lake had been considerably faster than driving. And despite the warming morning sun, the chill of wet clothes had his teeth beginning to chatter. As far as he was concerned, they couldn't tie the boat to the stone dock fast enough.

"While you go change into warm clothes," the General pointed toward a cluster of cabins, "we'll have Lucy put on a fresh pot of hot coffee and make you a good warm breakfast."

"That won't be necessary," he started, but the General raised his hand in a silencing gesture.

"Go," the older man ordered.

Rose smiled weakly at him. "You are beginning to take on a tinge of blue."

That he didn't doubt. "I guess I'd better go change. Thank you."

His two hosts turned and Rose sprinted up the hill past her grandfather. He wasn't sure what the next few days would hold, but if this morning was any indication, interesting might prove to be an understatement.

• • • •

Rose bolted up the porch steps two at a time. Stupid stupid stupid. Only on TV and in dumb movies did the apprentice fisherman literally hook a man. "Lucy!"

The porch door slammed shut behind her, reverberating through the entryway.

Carrying a basket of fabric strips, her grandmother's steps slowed. "Where's the fire?"

"More like who almost drowned."

"Oh heavens." Grams' eyes rounded wide. "Do I need to call 911?"

"No." Rose closed her eyes and slowly let out a deep breath. "Sorry Grams. I don't mean literally drowned. I mean I just dumped one of your guests into the lake."

This time her grandmother's brows shot up high, creasing her forehead like a shar-pei puppy. "Do I want to know how you managed that?"

Shaking her head, Rose continued toward the kitchen. "Let's just say it involved a stubborn general, a fishing pole, and seriously bad aim."

Keeping pace beside her, her grandmother's hand rose to her mouth in an effort to hide her amusement.

"It's not funny, Grams."

"No dear, I'm sure it wasn't."

"What isn't funny?" Lucy set the kettle on the stove and turned the flame up high.

"It seems our Rose has gone out of her way to make one of our guests feel welcome." Grams took a seat at the island, spreading the remnant strips from her unsuccessful attempt at quilting out beside her.

Lucy's gaze darted from one woman to the other and back. "I'm not sure I like the way you said that. Which guest?"

"Good question." Grams turned, facing Rose.

It occurred to her, with the embarrassing moment and limited conversation that followed, there had been no exchange of names on the boat. "I have no idea. Tall, dark hair, and an accent from the South, maybe Midwest, possibly Texas."

"Sounds like Mr. Buchanan. I think he's from Dallas. Checked in last night," Grams offered.

"If we were talking about Lily I might be worried." Lucy set an empty tea cup in front of Grams and reached for the whistling kettle. "Exactly what happened?"

"When you think about it," accompanied by his four-footed friends, the General entered the kitchen, "one might say it took quite a bit of skill to accomplish what you did."

"*What* did she do?" Lucy repeated

Between the chuckles, the snickers, and occasional guffaws, it took Rose a few minutes longer than it should have to relay the morning's events.

"All I can say," Lucy grinned unrepentantly, "is that you can't blame this one on me."

Now that she thought about it, if Rose didn't know better, this crazy man-catching escapade actually did have Lucy's fingerprints all over it. "Anyway, the General wants us to bring the man a good hot breakfast."

"Makes sense to me." Lucy nodded. "One breakfast tray coming up."

"Better add an extra thermos of hot coffee," the General said. "I suspect he's going to need it."

"And while you guys take care of our guest, I'm going to go change my clothes too."

"What's wrong with your clothes, dear?" Grams asked.

"Let's just say they're feeling a bit fishy." What the rest of the day called for was shorts and a t-shirt—not a reminder of the morning splash—and a good book. Whatever business she was responsible for could wait one more day.

"I'll let you know when Mr. Buchanan's breakfast is ready."

"Not me," she called over her shoulder. It would be perfectly fine if she never saw that man, or anything to remind her of her mortifying experience, again.

"Young lady," the General bellowed and Rose's shoulders sank.

"Hey." She walked past her grandfather, pausing to kiss him on the cheek. "I've already dumped the guy in the lake. Don't you think that's enough for one day?"

The General merely shook his head and mumbled, "You make it sound like you single handedly sank a battleship."

Perhaps she was overreacting just a tad. The man was a fisherman after all. Fishermen stood in water all the time. Didn't they? The sooner she got upstairs, into fresh clothes and a good long book, the better she'd feel.

"Why do you look so pensive?" Poppy came through the front door with a little less vigor than Rose had recently done and came to a stop at the foot of the stairs.

"Nothing really, just thinking I should have stayed in bed this morning."

"Oh, my. One of those days? Do I want to know what happened?"

Rose shook her head and waved her thumb over her shoulder at the kitchen. "Go on inside. I'm sure Lucy will be glad to tell you all about it."

Poppy tipped her head up at her cousin and scrunched her face. "Maybe we should just both play hooky today."

"You too?"

"The church's board of directors are meeting later this morning. Whenever there's a new project on the agenda things never go well."

Rose laughed. "Don't we make quite the pair. Sounds like we might need a night to swap reports over s'mores and a bottle of red wine."

"Oh, I like the sound of that!" Her cousin's mood immediately brightened. "I'm not sure if I can make it tonight, but definitely tomorrow!"

"Works for me." It had been ages since she'd sat at the lake with her cousins and made s'mores.

"Deal." Grinning, Poppy flashed a thumbs up and hurried off to the kitchen.

Already today was looking up. All she had to do was steer clear of Mr. Buchanan for the next few days and all would be well. With a few hundred fishermen descending on Lake Lawford for the tournament, how hard could it be to avoid one long tall Texan?

CHAPTER FOUR

For all the rustic appearance of the cabins, the place was not short on creature comforts. At this moment the cabin's tankless hot water heater was top on his appreciation list. The feather-soft bed followed, but the to-die-for breakfast was quickly edging the hot water out of first place.

When the General had insisted he have a hot meal after fishing him out of the lake, he'd expected a couple of eggs, bacon and toast or muffins. The young brunette he'd crossed paths with last night had delivered a meal suitable for a five-star hotel. The omelet was light enough to float off the plate, the pan-fried potatoes were golden brown, the bacon cooked to perfection, and if the biscuits and jams weren't homemade he'd eat his favorite hat. It was going to take an extra-long workout to burn off the calories he'd consumed. Since the archaic internet system, about as effective as two tin cans and a string, prohibited him killing time on his laptop or his games, and Hart Land didn't come equipped with a gym, now was a good time for a walk. A long walk. He'd take in the scenery, then check in at the main house to see if anyone could take him to pick up his rental car. Good plan for the rest of the morning.

According to the brochures on the counter, the property had several paths that led up the mountain as well as lakefront beaches suitable for strolling. Phone in hand, he glanced around the cabin debating if he should bring his laptop and find a comfortable spot to tinker with his latest project, only to remind himself he was supposed to be unplugging. Even though the idea had been to relax with his grandfather, he still held out hope that he wouldn't be here alone the entire trip. Closing the door behind him, he turned left and headed for the shore.

Right about now, if he'd been home in Texas instead of enjoying cool morning breezes, he'd be baking in the hot sun or enjoying the cool morning air conditioning. The fresh air certainly had refrigerated air beat hands down. Taking in deep breaths and keeping his eyes toward the shore, he resisted the urge to reach for his phone. This whole unplugging thing might prove to be harder than he thought without his grandfather's conversation to help pass the time.

Halfway to the water, he noticed several people gathering on the grassy dock area where the General had tied the boat this morning. It looked like he wasn't the only one appreciating the pleasant summer weather. Kids already were slapping at the tetherball, and adults laughed and pitched horseshoes. Maybe later he'd wander over and see if strangers were welcome, but right now, the quiet, pristine flow and lack of activity on the water called to him.

Not till he'd stood on the low brick wall by the sand did he realize he wasn't the only one appreciating the morning solitude. "Hello again."

From under a large brimmed floppy hat, big green eyes blinked wide at him. "Hello."

Not the warmest greeting he'd ever heard. "Any good?"

A deep crease formed between the pretty redhead's brows.

He lifted his chin, pointing to the massive hardback in her hands.

"Oh! Actually, yes. It's been eons since I've had the time to read anything that didn't have instructions or require editing."

Quickly his mind ran through possibilities of a career that involved both instructions and editing. "Spec writer?"

Those brows buckled again. "Excuse me?"

"Sorry." He shook his head. "I forget there is a world outside IT. What is it that you do that requires both instructions and editing?"

She shifted a long paper bookmark toward the front pages and closed the cover. "I'm a curator at the Central Boston Museum for the Arts."

Wow. "I'm not sure which is more impressive, the job or that massive book you're reading. I mean, besides the fact that I figured everyone on vacation carried a library of reading on a digital device, I didn't think anyone wrote books that big anymore."

"First," she smiled up at him, "I like the feel of paper between my fingers. It makes the story seem more real. And as for the size," her eyes twinkled, "that could be because Tolstoy wrote *Anna Karenina* over a hundred years ago."

"Okay. Now I am truly impressed." He waved at the empty space beside her. "May I?"

The way her eyes closed for a fraction longer than a blink and her chest heaved with the intake of a deep breath, he thought she was searching for a polite way to say *get lost buddy.*

Prepared to let her off the hook, he barely opened his mouth to speak when she pointed to a distant spot behind him. "Feel free to pull up a chair."

Looking over his shoulder, he saw a stack of lounge chairs piled near the stone dock. Not sure if accepting would be an imposition, he took a moment to study her eyes. The downside of working with programming and computers most of his days meant reading people was not his strong suit. On the other hand, he still had enough old-fashioned Texas training to feel confident in a quick assessment that her offer was sincere. "Thank you."

While he retrieved and dragged one of the chairs over to her side, she slowly scanned the lake, her gaze finally settling on the activity behind them. "You probably have another hour at best before the remaining chairs will be scooped up by guests and scattered across the Point and the beach."

"Point?" Angling the chair slightly, he straddled it and faced her.

She gestured to the stone dock behind her. "The Point is what we call that strip of land. A few great-grandfathers ago, the family built that area extending our property."

The area she referred to was long enough and wide enough to build a good size house on if someone wanted. "That's quite a bit of extension."

"Yes. And we love it. Property owners aren't allowed to build out into the lake anymore so we're one of the few that have a stone dock like that. It's great for playing games, for sunbathing, or tying a boat to. As you already know from this morning." A hint of blush pinkened her cheeks. "Which, by the way, I really am sorry about."

"No further apologies needed. Getting a little wet is all part of lake life and fishing."

Her face brightened in what he suspected was the first true smile he'd seen from her. "I think today qualified as more than *a little* wet."

"Perhaps." He truly had been drenched. "But I'm not being polite when I say that's not the first time I've taken a fall in a body of water."

She nodded. "Okay. I'll buy that."

"Good, because some of those times make me very grateful that everybody and their godmother wasn't running around back then with cell phones taking pictures and videos of our most embarrassing moments."

"Really?" She set the book she'd been cradling down on the sand beside her. "Sounds like you have a few stories to tell."

"Oh no." Pinching his thumb and forefinger together, he slid them from one side of his mouth to the other. "My lips are sealed."

"Too bad," she chuckled. "It might have been more entertaining than Tolstoy."

"Rest assured, most of my life story would put you to sleep."

The corners of her mouth lifted in another heartfelt grin. "Maybe, but what about the least?"

Touché. Beautiful *and* smart. Maybe being hooked and soaked wasn't such a bad way to start his day after all.

• • • •

Now that Rose had a good looking guy at her side who didn't appear to have any early warning signs of blatant jerk, she wasn't sure she knew what to do with him. That thought gave her pause. She could schmooze a donor out of a year's salary, but presented with a friendly, possibly flirting, single adult male…her gaze shot to his left hand…probably single male, she was at a loss for words. "Tell me, Mr. Buchanan, what is it you do with IT?"

"According to my brothers I'm nothing more than a computer geek, but the official job description is software developer, and please call me Logan." He cocked his head to one side. "I don't remember giving my last name."

That made her laugh. "Small town, big family."

"Of course." He smothered a low chuckle.

The low throaty rumble sent a shiver skittering up her spine. Picking up a nearby tube of sunscreen, she used it as an excuse to brush away the reaction. "How are you adapting to our unplugged lifestyle?"

"Slowly." His gaze momentarily drifted over his shoulder toward his cabin. "I may have a slight case of high-speed internet withdrawal."

She held back a smile. If ordinary guests struggled to unplug from their phones and computers, she could only imagine how unnerved he might be feeling away from his technology. "Do you come from a small town?"

"Not exactly. I grew up on a ranch outside of Dallas. Most days it felt like living in the middle of nowhere, but in reality the property line is only thirty minutes outside of sprawling suburbia. Still, we did most of our business in the smaller neighboring towns."

"Sounds a bit like me. Born and raised in Boston, but spent my summers up here. Rockwell might as well have been depicting life in Lawford. It's hard to imagine that I could love living in two opposing ends of the spectrum so much, but I do."

"I know what you mean. Sitting at a keyboard in a cubicle in one of the fastest growing cities in the country is diametrically opposed to big skies and ranch life." His gaze lingered on the water. Dark brown eyes with flecks of golden brown shimmered when he smiled.

"Have you always been a fisherman?" she asked.

Those golden flecks sparkled and danced as his cheeks lifted, flashing the perfect smile. "Ever since my grandfather put a fishing rod in my hand by the creek."

"And the tournaments?"

"That took longer. My grandfather is military. Once he retired, I was the only grandson that actually enjoyed fishing *and* competition."

"When my grandfather got the idea to help Cindy raise money for the wildlife center with a fishing tournament, and then asked me to help with the fundraising end of this project, I thought one little tournament couldn't be that hard. Then I looked up fishing tournaments and was blown away at the statistics. The sheer numbers of participants was mind boggling. Made me wonder what the big deal was. Should have realized it's a testosterone thing."

"Not necessarily. I know some pretty good fishermen who aren't men."

She bobbed her head. Wasn't that the truth for every typically male dominated career.

For the third or fourth time in the last hour of conversation, Logan checked his watch. This time he made a tsking sound and pushed to his feet. "I wish I could chat longer but I need to find the General about picking up my rental."

"Oh." Of course. How could she have forgotten that part. Grabbing her book, she stood as well. "I can take you."

His glum expression slid away, followed by a lazy smile that threatened to give her goosebumps again. "If it's not inconvenient."

She caught herself before laughing off the statement. "It's the least I can do."

"There you are." The General strolled up to them, two dogs at his sides. "Lunch is about to be served."

Lady and Sarge trotted up to Logan, sniffing his shoes, then lifting their heads to sniff at his knees, his pockets, over to his elbow and down his arms before licking his hands. Immediately getting down on his haunches, putting himself at eye level with the pups, Logan grinned and scratched behind their ears. The guy not only was proving he wasn't a jerk, he was doing a good job of racking up the nice guy points.

"Whole house smells like corned beef," the General continued, "which means we'll be having Katie's soda bread. Don't want to be late for that. Afterward, I'll be happy to take you to get your car."

"We were just discussing his car," Rose spoke up. How silly was it that the change of plans had left her rather disappointed. She was going to have to stop behaving like such a girl. Determined to avoid the man at any cost one minute and then disappointed at losing time with him the next.

"Good. We can discuss it more over lunch." It wasn't exactly an order, but as grandchildren of military men, neither of them was about to argue with the retired Marine corps general.

Less than half an hour later, the dining room was full with both family and friends.

"I've heard so much lately about your grandfather. Was looking forward to meeting him." Their neighbor Ralph stabbed at a boiled potato. "And, of course, beating his Annapolis as…er, butt, in cards."

"Really?" Logan looked up, curiosity in his gaze.

The General cleared his throat. "I may have mentioned him a time or two since the reunion."

"Yes." Logan cut into his corned beef. "He told me a whole bunch of you reconnected."

"I don't know about a whole bunch," the General mumbled.

Logan hefted one shoulder in a lazy shrug. "Well, I know he's extremely excited about seeing you in Florida this fall."

"Florida?" Rose's fork froze halfway to her mouth. Surely her grandparents weren't planning on joining what northerners often teased to be Southern New York's retirement population. Her heart did a nose dive to her stomach. What would Hart Land be without the General and Grams?

"Yes." Grams patted her granddaughter's hand. "We had such a lovely time at the reunion. Since so many of your grandfather's friends have retired there, we're working out details for an informal smaller gathering in warmer weather this winter. I think it will be lovely."

Relief washed over her. One vacation in winter wouldn't be so bad. Not that she got much opportunity to spend a whole lot of time at the lake, winter or any other time, but knowing her grandparents were here if she did was an enormous comfort. She didn't want to even consider the time when they would no longer be around. Which brought a totally different thought to mind. This morning on the lake, even dealing with worms had been enjoyable. As had reading on the beach. There had to be some way to do her job and get away to be with family more often.

"Everything okay?" Logan asked softly, leaning closer.

Those blasted shivers struck, threatening goosebumps again, and she had no idea if she was anything close to okay.

CHAPTER FIVE

"**O**h, I almost forgot." Grams pushed away from the table. "Martha called earlier and said she talked their mother into parting with their great-grandmother's trunk. It might need a little cleaning up as it's been gathering dust in the attic for decades, but Mabel also agreed you could have whatever you find inside that isn't family specific, and Martha says you'd better go pick it up now before Mabel changes her mind."

"All right." Rose turned to her grandfather. "Can I borrow the jeep?"

"Sure, but you're going to need some help loading. I'll see if George has time to spare."

"I have time," Logan spit out. "I mean, other than picking up my car and riding around the lake, my slate is clear."

"Maybe," her grandmother leaned forward, "you should take advantage of Mr. Buchanan's generosity with his time and do a round of donation pick-ups?"

"Not a bad idea." She nodded, running the list through her mind again. "But if that's the case we might need to borrow George's truck."

"Excellent plan," her grandfather agreed, his eyes smiling.

"I'd better take a minute to change." She shoved her chair away from the table. Shorts and a t-shirt might work under a shade tree by the beach, but not if they wound up rummaging through anyone's attic. "I'll be back in a jiffy."

Hurrying up the stairs, she pushed away thoughts of what to wear that wouldn't make her look like a country mouse and focus on her list of donors. They'd lucked out with some fantastic items but as she reached the top of the stairs her mind returned to circling around what would look businesslike, but casual, but flattering, but routine, and of course, flattering. In the end, she'd settled for layering of beige and tan from her shoes and slacks to her blouse and earrings. Not too severe, not too formal, and just enough casual to fit in with the lake or trudging through attics and storage rooms. And of course, the neutral shades were very flattering to her red hair. Not that it should matter. Pulling the binder out from between the matching bookends, she double-checked the section with donations and thanked the heavens once again for Sarah. On the top of the purple coded donation section, Sarah had left a detailed spreadsheet in list form. This would make keeping track of pickups easy for Rose. Well, easier.

"There she is." At the bottom of the stairs her grandfather looked up from chatting with Ralph and Logan.

Was it her imagination or did Logan's eyes light up at the sight of her? *No*. She had to be imagining things. Channeling all that concern over a flattering wardrobe. Still, what was it about *this* guy in particular that had her regressing to thinking like a teenage girl?

His gaze shifted to the small binder against her breast and his eyes widened for a fraction of a moment before a calm smile covered up his surprise. "Ready?"

"Ready." Falling into step beside him, she waved at her grandfather and his friend and began mentally tallying the order of donors and reflected on the spark of surprise in his eyes. If he thought reading Tolstoy was a big deal, she could only imagine his reaction if he saw the binder thrice as thick as this one for the upcoming show at the museum.

"Where are we going?" he asked as he held the door for her.

"We should start at the top of the list. That one is the furthest away and then we can double back through town until we run out of room in the truck."

"That much stuff?" Logan whistled, holding the car door this time. Nice guy *and* an old-school gentleman. The perfect combo.

"Oh, yeah. We've had some very nice donations come in from all over the mountain, but the locals have been especially generous. This wildlife center for conservation, rehabilitation, and education is not only my cousin Cindy's pet project," she chuckled, "no pun intended, it means a great deal to anyone who loves this mountain."

His gaze shifted to the trees along the route as they turned out of Hart Land. "I can understand that. The ranch has a lot of flat, and not a lot of green, and limited wildlife, but the land has been in our family for generations. You can't replace history, and it's our responsibility to preserve the history, the land, and everything that lives on it."

"I couldn't agree more. That's why I let my grandfather rope me into this whole thing." She drove by the Pastry Stop and pointed. "By the way, that's my cousin Lily's bakery."

"Responsible for today's dessert?"

"The one and only."

"I might have to do a little window shopping while we're here."

Rose smiled. "I gather you have a sweet tooth?"

"You mean the two large helpings I had didn't give it away?"

"That may have been my first clue." She laughed. "But pretty much everyone in this family has a sweet tooth thanks to Lily."

"If that chocolate cake was any indication, I can certainly understand why. Though I freely admit I may be addicted to those crescent almond cookies."

"You wouldn't be the only one. I'm torn between the almonds and the spitzbuben. Not that I'd refuse anything Lily baked." Coming up on the narrow dirt road that led to the first stop, she took a sharp turn and bounced up the hill.

"I sure hope whatever we're picking up isn't breakable."

"Well, if the trunk hasn't broken apart in the last century, I think it will make it to the Inn today.

Five stops later, and a half full pickup bed, next on her list of donors was Edna from Buy the Book. Logan followed her into the quaint shop. All conversation stopped at first sight of what many considered hallowed walls. Stacks and stacks of books were displayed on solid wood shelves handcrafted at least 100 years ago. Edna had salvaged them when the original mountain library was torn down. In the back, protected in more handcrafted, glass fronted cabinets, classic first editions of well-loved books, including *Gone With the Wind* and *To Kill a Mockingbird* were available for sale.

"Oh my." His fingers gravitated towards the case, stopping short at touching the glass. "Never really got *Gone With the Wind*, but for the longest time *To Kill a Mockingbird* was one of my favorite books."

She didn't know why that surprised her. After all, people in Texas did read. Didn't they? Of course they did. One more plus for the nice, polite guy. "One of mine too."

"Here you go!" Edna came hurrying out from her office behind the counter. "This struck me as a good fit for the event."

Rose had to snap her mouth shut. She'd expected a series from some popular author. Or perhaps an autographed copy of a book by some well-known fishermen, if something like that even existed. But she hadn't expected this. "*Tom Sawyer*." She didn't have to open the cover to know that Edna was donating a first edition of the famed Mark Twain novel. Fishing did have its place in the classic novel and something about a simpler way of a lifestyle long gone brought home the value of preserving the animal life and land around them. "On behalf of Cindy and the wildlife center, thank you."

Logan hadn't said more than two words once Edna presented them with *The Adventures of Tom Sawyer* for the auction. Curiosity had her wondering what had suddenly made him so quiet. "Penny for your thoughts?"

The Hart Land guest stood in front of the bookstore and looked up the street. "My grandfather, the one who's friends with your grandfather, is my mom's dad. She had a brother, my uncle Bill. He was killed in a friendly fire accident when I was in high school."

"I know it was a long time ago, but I'm sorry for your loss."

"Thanks. Uncle Bill was a fan of Mark Twain. When he'd come to visit, we would go down by the creek. Of course, in Texas it's not much of a creek, but enough to keep this one weeping willow tree growing. My brothers and I would lean back against the big old trunk and Uncle Bill would help us drop a line into the creek. Not a fancy fishing rod, but a stick that we picked out ourselves and he'd help fashion into a fishing rod. Then we'd wait for a fish to bite and listen to him read from a Mark Twain book."

"That sounds like a wonderful memory."

He bobbed his head. "It was. By the time I was ten we'd graduated from a hand-hewn stick to a real fishing pole—not that we ever caught any fish in that little creek. My brothers had grown tired of Mark Twain, but Uncle Bill and I continued the tradition for three more years. We were no longer reading Mark Twain, but that didn't matter."

"I know this sounds silly, but I think I really like your Uncle Bill." *And maybe his nephew too.*

• • • •

Why a single copy of Tom Sawyer had made Logan so sentimental, he couldn't say. Maybe it was that he hadn't really thought of Uncle Bill for quite some time. Or maybe it's because he hadn't read *Tom Sawyer* since he was 11 years old. But he was glad to have relived those memories for even a few minutes. And even more pleased to have done so with the pretty redhead who would read *Anna Karenina* for pleasure.

Still standing by the car in front of the quaint bookstore, his gaze drifted across the street. A few shops up, he noticed a sign for the village creamery. "Would I be in the money if I were to bet that the ice cream parlor across the street sells homemade ice cream?"

"You would." A broad grin took over her face to match the impish glint in her eyes. "Depending on how much money you wagered."

Everything about this woman made him want to grin like a fool and never stop. "Do we have time for a taste?"

"Absolutely. Not only is it criminal to visit downtown Lawford without stopping at the village creamery, I think it's very fitting for the memory of your uncle and Tom Sawyer to indulge in a little afternoon refreshment."

He resisted the urge to snatch her hand in his and skip across the street like a couple of kids channeling Becky Thatcher and Tom Sawyer. "Do you have a favorite flavor?"

"I suppose *all of them* is not the answer you're looking for?"

A woman after his own heart. He bit back a smile. "Works for me"

Small wrought iron tables with two matching round back chairs assured the inside of the parlor to be everything he would have expected. The pastel colors dressing the walls and the pictures depicting a simpler time and place hanging prominently near the entry added to the brief journey back in time. The entire feeling matched everything he'd noticed today on Main Street, from the beauty parlor with the big old-fashioned hairdryers to the barbershop pole twirling on the sidewalk making sure any passerby knew this was the place to come in for a trim or a shave or just as important, friendly conversation. He had no doubt that the conversation would come with an old-fashioned shave with heated towels, warm lather, and maybe even a single edge blade. He might have to stop in and see for himself.

"I lost you." Rose waved at him. "Thinking of your uncle again?"

His fingers mindlessly ran from his cheek down his jawline. "Actually, I was thinking about the barber shop."

"Floyd's?"

How had he not noticed the shop was named Floyd's. "Really?"

Rose chuckled loud enough for the sales clerk to look up from elbow deep in a creamy tub of butter pecan. "Yes, really. But it's a long story."

"Now you have my curiosity aroused."

Smiling at the clerk in front of her, Rose tapped on the glass case. "Morning, Annabelle. That looks wonderful. I'll have the butter pecan. Single scoop in a cone."

"And you, sir?" the young girl asked.

"I'll have the butter pecan as well. But make mine a double." He nodded at the young lady and turned to Rose. "This way there'll be time for you to tell me the story of Floyd's."

She laughed again. He liked the sound of it. He was liking a lot of things about today. Even the dunk in the water this morning didn't seem to be nearly as brisk or inconvenient as it had felt at the time.

By the time she'd finished relaying the stories of how the barbershop had gotten its name, the afternoon checker games much like those seen on retro TV for decades, and how the beauty parlor found its owner, Logan was beginning to understand why his grandfather had been so taken by a town he'd only visited once or twice.

Resisting the urge to wipe away a tiny drip of melted ice cream lingering at the corner of her mouth, he opted to merely hand her a napkin and then point to the same spot on his own face. The decision seemed the safer choice than actually allowing himself to touch her, however innocently. "Where to now?"

"It's getting a little late." She glanced at her phone, then reached into her canvas and extracted the binder that she had lugged from donor to donor. "I think we've done enough for today. You've been a big help. I hadn't really taken into account how heavy a refurbished steamer trunk could be."

"Honestly, I had never taken a steamer trunk into account at all." He watched as she flipped the binder and meticulously checked off several boxes on one of the pages before initialing it and closing the cover. "Wouldn't that be easier on a tablet or even your phone?"

She shrugged. "I actually do have a great deal of this on computer. Even though I own a tablet, I find it more bulky to deal with."

"More bulky than an 8 x 11 binder?"

"Let's just say, it's a bit like the book thing. I like the feel of actual paper. I prefer flipping a page than giving myself carpal tunnel scrolling on a screen. And quite frankly," she slid the binder back in place, and stood, "if the unthinkable happened and the Internet collapsed for a day, or even an hour, me and my binder would be on top of the world."

"I love a good book as much as the next guy, but thank you very much, I'll trust my computer over hand computations any day of the week." Even though the odds of the cyber world as they knew it completely falling off the face of the earth for even a minute was completely out of the question, just the mere mention of the possibility made him cringe. "I seriously hope your confidence is never tested. I don't even want to consider what would happen to everybody if the Internet and all its electronic connections simply disappeared."

Chuckling, she led the way to the door. "Imagine, people might actually have to speak to each other if they couldn't text." She held the door open for him. "Or schools would have to teach cursive so people could write love letters again."

He followed her out the door, rolling his eyes. "Why do I have a feeling you're about to give me a very long list of why the world would be better off without technology?"

"Because you strike me as a very smart man who catches on quickly." That lovely smile of hers would be incredibly easy to get very attached to. "Do you want the whole list or just some of it?"

Letting his head fall back, he barked out a laugh from deep down in his chest. The ride back to Hart House might prove to be the most interesting part of his day yet.

CHAPTER SIX

"**M**an, this house always smells so good at dinnertime." Lily's husband Cole crossed the expansive kitchen and gave his flour covered wife a kiss on the cheek.

Lucy glanced up from the pot she was stirring. "Normally I'd give your wife the credit, but since the biscuits haven't got in the oven yet, I'm giving all of today's credit to my gravy."

"I've known a lot of Italian grandmother's gravy that can't compete with yours," Grant said as he came through the doorway, holding hands with Rose's sister Violet.

Violet sniffed the air, then wrapped each person in the room with a spine straightening hug. "I knew it was worth leaving Boston early."

"Oh, this is a lovely surprise." Grams set the bundle of fabric braids aside to hug Violet and her fiancé, then turned to Lucy. "Did you know they were coming?"

Lucy shook her head. "I expected that nice Mr. Buchanan would be joining us for dinner and I thought he might appreciate a good Yankee-made spaghetti sauce."

"Such a shame he's having to work." Grams sat back down in her spot.

Rose shrugged. After having spent such an enjoyable afternoon she was a bit disappointed when the call came in from his boss in Texas. "I think if his grandfather, Captain Amlin, had been here, he might have passed the problem off to the next guy."

"Captain Amlin?" Cole's chin tucked against his neck and his brows dipped in thought. "I wonder if that's the same Captain Amlin my grandfather knows."

Grant spun about to face Cole. "My grandfather has a friend with that name too. They all went to Annapolis together."

Pausing from kneading, Lily looked to her husband and her cousins before her gaze settled on the men in front of her. "Wait a minute. Did I know that your grandfathers went to Annapolis?"

"If you did," Violet followed Lily's gaze, "you know more than me."

"What's your grandfather's name?" Grant asked Cole.

"Captain Donald McIntyre," Cole responded.

"I'll have to ask if my grandfather knows him."

"Same here." Cole nodded. "Though McIntyre isn't that uncommon."

"Nope, but you know how the brass always seem to know each other." Grant cocked his head to one side. "First time I ran into Jake, he recognized my grandfather's name. Annapolis can be a small world."

"Especially after that big reunion last year," Cole added.

That caught Rose's attention. She glanced at her grandmother studiously working on her project, almost oblivious to the conversation. Nothing unusual as the woman was always devoting herself to a new hobby, though this time she seemed particularly engrossed in the beginnings of her rag rug. And Lucy, who always had something to say about everything, had conveniently stepped outside to feed Sadie and the new stray they'd sort of adopted.

"The same reunion the General went to?" Lily asked.

"That's what I was wondering." Rose once again looked to her grandmother, still braiding away. "Do these names ring a bell, Grams?"

Fiona Hart lifted her head. "I'm sorry, dear, what? These darn seams keep turning out, doesn't seem to look right. Perhaps I'm trying too hard."

"Trying too hard to what?" Lucy came through the back door, a large aluminum dish in her hands.

"This just doesn't look right." Grams held up the long string of fabric strips she'd sewn together and now carefully had spent hours braiding. Rose didn't even want to think how her less than nimble-fingered grandmother was going to adhere those braids into a rug. At least not one that resembled a circle.

Lucy sighed. "I think you should go back to the painting. I liked those stones."

"The quilted trivets are nice," Lily added.

"They do seem to come in handy." Grams smiled, the crease between her brow disappearing.

"Good grief." Poppy rushed into the room. Instead of her usual bubbly cheer, she gave her grandmother a peck on the cheek, and dropped into the chair beside her. "For God fearing Christians, sometimes the church board of directors can be real jerks."

"Uh oh." Lucy turned off the water and stilled with the filled bowl in her hand. "What happened?"

"Just another argument over whether or not to start a Mother's Day Out program. I've never been happier to see a day come to an end. I didn't even have time for lunch. I am seriously ready to eat whatever smells so good."

"Whatever?" Lily looked up. "It's Lucy's gravy."

"Oh, man. Now I'm really hungry." Poppy made a half-hearted effort to push to her feet.

"You stay put." Violet finished tying the apron behind her back. "We got this, and like you, I'm ready to put some food on those quilted trivets. Is the table set?"

"Not yet," Lily answered.

"I'll get the dishes." Grant turned on his heel, winked at Violet, and headed for the cupboard.

Cole bobbed his head. "I'll get the silverware."

Both men were as much at home in the household as the women who were raised there. It was nice to see. As a matter of fact, it was nice to see so many of her cousins one by one finding guys who made them truly happy. The dating world was so full of clueless buffoons, self-centered morons, or just plain boring men, she hadn't thought about finding a lifelong mate in ages. Maybe when she got back to Boston she should look into one of those online dating apps. Not that her cousins had needed matchmaking technology. They seemed to have done just fine without anyone's help.

• • • •

From day one, Logan had told his supervisors the deadline was unrealistic. With so much support coming from across the world in a completely different time zone, there simply was not enough time for everyone to work together. Never mind push the new product out to the real world. At least he was able to fix the more pressing complication with a few minor code changes, but if they expected him to resolve the other issues, they were simply going to have to wait until after this week.

Whether his grandfather joined him or not, he'd already enjoyed the start of this vacation more than any he could remember since he was a kid. There was no way he was letting the real world get in the way. Of course it hadn't hurt that the call with his boss had dropped three times in less than fifteen minutes, allowing him to claim he simply did not have the bandwidth needed to be much help. He wasn't about to suggest he could probably find some place to work from with a reasonable high speed Internet connection, if not in Lawford proper, in a bigger nearby town.

Having the best Internet connection from the large rocker of the front porch had turned out to be the one bright side to spending the last few hours on his computer. Sending off his last email to his counterpart across the world, he signed off and closed the laptop. Everyone was now officially, and truly, on their own. If they couldn't figure this mess out without him, well they were just SOL.

The downside to having spent all this time on his porch was that he'd missed dinner at the big house and hadn't really prepared anything on his own. Though he noticed the refrigerator came stocked with basics. He could probably scramble some eggs, or throw a sandwich together. Neither of which sounded terribly appetizing after having been spoiled with a large breakfast and a delicious lunch with the Hart family. Beggars couldn't be choosers. Maybe he should just take a ride into town and try out the diner with the big pink neon sign. Greasy spoons and small towns were known for great food—usually. It might be worth taking a chance on.

"Done with work, or just taking a break?" The soft voice from over his shoulder was a welcome change. The delicious aromas blowing his way from the tray Rose held in her hand made his stomach rumble. Only one day eating Hart food and already he'd turned into Pavlov's dog, salivating at the sight of a dinner tray.

Though it was definitely the sight of the redheaded messenger that was making his heart race. "This is a nice surprise."

"If there's one thing in this world that Lucy loves more than matchmaking, it's feeding people."

He'd actually meant her arrival, not the food, but it was probably best he not correct her. "Is this another one of those long stories like Floyd the barber and Betty the hairdresser?"

Rose laughed. "You might say that. The short version is Lucy thinks of herself as Hello Dolly. Has the song on her phone as a ring tone and creates havoc anytime she makes any effort to hook two people up. That's all I'm saying. Well, that and she hasn't burned the house down yet."

For a woman who had serious taste in reading and a job that not just any slouch could do, especially not at her young age, she had an entertaining way of turning a phrase to leave anyone wanting more. He certainly felt that way, and about more than just her stories.

"If you haven't eaten yet, spaghetti is still warm." Balancing the tray on her hip, she lifted the cloth covering the meal high enough for him to see the covered dish, the bread which he guessed was homemade, a dessert he couldn't quite make out but looked good enough to make his stomach rumble again—this time more loudly, and the piece de resistance, a cold beer. "I grabbed one of the General's favorite beers on my way out the door. Sort of an extra thank you for not biting my head off this morning and all your help this afternoon."

"As far as a peace offering goes, this was pretty good. It'll just hit the spot."

She flashed him another of those smiles worthy of a toothpaste commercial that set his heart racing once again. "Shall I put this inside or leave it here?"

"Oh." He set the laptop down and pushed to his feet, reaching for the tray. "Let me."

"It's okay. I've got it. Where do you want it?"

"Here on this table will be fine. If you'll join me, I hate to eat alone." Did that sound as needy to her as it did to him? Or as lame? Didn't most single adults eat alone these days.

"I've already eaten but never turn down an offer to enjoy a nice view of the lake."

Anything that kept her here longer worked for him. "I'm not sure what else there is to drink in the fridge."

She lifted the cover on the other side of the tray, displaying a second beverage. "Just in case." One corner of her mouth tipped up in a sly grin.

"Shall I get a glass?" he asked through his own amusement.

"Only if you want one."

He raised a brow at her, but remained silent.

"Yeah." Her soft chuckle was as pleasant as her smile. "You didn't look like the glass kind of guy."

"Does it count if my grandmother would only drink her beer from a glass? Preferably tall and chilled."

Her shoulders bounced as her chuckle grew into a sweet laugh. "Definitely counts."

For the next few minutes they adjusted porch furniture. He dragged the table to the other side of his rocker, and she inched it closer then moved the second rocker at an angle to face the lake. By the time she was done, the porch was staged perfectly to almost face each other and still get the perfect evening views.

"So you're not just this way with trucks and antiques."

Rose set her chair rocking and laughed. "We never would have fit everything in the truck if we'd done it your way."

"My way wasn't that bad." He stabbed at a forkful of pasta.

"No, not at all. Especially when you came within inches of tossing the bird cage onto a hundred year old oil painting."

"Did you get a good look at the thing? Trust me, I was doing you a favor."

Shaking her head, she bit back another laugh. "That from a man who handled a stuffed fish with the care of a newborn babe."

He swallowed another bite of the best pasta dinner he'd ever had. "That wasn't just a fish, it was a blue marlin. Do you have any idea how much these fishermen are likely to pay for that?"

"Apparently more than a twentieth century landscape in oils."

This time he laughed. "See? You're catching on." Truth was she'd packed that truck so neat and tight, had she said she moonlighted for a moving company, he'd have believed her.

"I certainly hope you're right about that fish." Lifting her heel, she set her chair rocking.

"On this, trust me. And get used to saying marlin." Practically having inhaled his dinner, he swallowed the last bite. "Perfect."

"Lucy's pasta and gravy. Totally."

"Agreed, totally, but so is the night. I can't remember the last time a summer evening was filled with pleasant temperatures and stunning views."

"Let's hope it stays that way." Her gaze scanned the distance

"What's wrong?"

"Nothing yet, but forecasters are predicting a nasty storm to blow in. I just hope they're wrong and it stays away till after the tournament.

"Ditto." Empty plate in hand, he stood. "Would you like some coffee?"

"Actually, that would be great." She followed him into the kitchen and headed straight for the coffee pot.

"I can do that." He pulled two mugs from the cabinet and waved one at her.

"I know, but I'm happy to do it."

He considered that for just a moment and decided if the woman made coffee with the same efficiency she loaded a truck and not the way she cast a fishing rod, he'd be better off giving in. "Thanks."

"How do you take it?" She reached for the sugar bowl.

He pulled the milk from the fridge. "Milk and sugar."

"Regular it is."

From behind the counter in the compact kitchen, he watched her pour out the coffee, noticing she used milk like him but skipped the sugar. Such a silly little thing but it pleased him to learn something new about the General's granddaughter. He was most definitely enjoying learning more about Rose. So far everything about her had been teetering between simply interesting and absolutely fascinating. How long could he drag out drinking a single cup of coffee was the question at hand.

CHAPTER SEVEN

Today was proving to be a major improvement over yesterday. At least fish wise. In search of the sweet spot for the tourney, he'd spent most of yesterday morning and midday on the lake, moving from one disappointing location to another. Not even the delicious boxed brunch Lucy had dropped off or the pleasure of enjoying the meal under a massive willow that brought him back once again to his days with his uncle on the ranch had helped. To his chagrin, much like the creek back home, the fish didn't seem to appreciate the peaceful locale as much as he had.

The plan for his evening hadn't gone any better. Walking to his cabin after his poor day of fishing, he'd noticed Rose working at a card table on the huge wrap around porch at the main house. Surrounded by stacks of papers and a phone perched between her shoulder and her ear, he could only imagine the amount of behind the scenes work she had on her plate. He'd attended many a fishing tournament, some of the biggest in the country even, but only a few had a fundraiser gala attached to it and most of those had a lot more help than one museum curator and a retired general and his family. Despite being the perfect opportunity on the surface for a casual visit, he knew she was short on time and most likely didn't need the interruption. To resist the temptation of stopping and talking to her, he'd decided to take a few notes on a new idea that had popped into his head while waiting for the fish. There'd be another chance to visit tonight when he took the General up on his invitation to join the family for cards on the porch. The wrench in his backup plans came when instead of merely jotting down some ideas, he began tinkering, losing all track of time. When he'd looked up from his work it was way past any reasonable hour to join in the family fun, never mind run into the smiling redhead.

This morning he decided to focus on two things only. Rose and the fish. He started by trying the fishing spot once again that Mrs.

Hart had suggested upon his arrival two days ago. He should have known to trust a loving grandmother, even if she wasn't *his* grandmother. Since this time he wasn't splashing around having been pulled into the water, the fish were darn happy to cooperate. He'd caught and released six good size bass, not including the few too small for legalities, keeping only one of his catch for a nice lunch.

If the plan was to cook his fish, he'd need a few more groceries than the basics the cottage stocked. For the short ride back to town, he'd debated taking advantage of the bare cupboards as an excuse to head to the main house and borrow the proverbial cup of sugar and hopefully run into Rose—his second agenda for the day—but a picture of her working on the porch yesterday came to mind, followed by his mother's voice urging him to be thoughtful of others. No matter how much he'd been itching to hear Rose's voice and laughter, he opted to stop by the local grocery instead.

"Top of the morning to you," a sweet voice called to him as he came through the door.

"Good morning."

"Been fishing, have you?"

He probably did look like a character from the Andy Griffith show, his favorite hat, the vest, and even though it wasn't made of flannel, his shirt was the stereotypical required plaid pattern. "The lake was good to me."

The woman smiled, and the light from the window beaming behind her gave her a surreal glow. She looked like the portrait of an angel worthy of hanging in any famous gallery. "Did you catch Old Blue?"

Walking down the aisle with miscellaneous dry goods, he paused to look up. "Old Blue?"

"Surely someone has mentioned Blue to you."

He grabbed a jar of minced garlic and shook his head. "Can't say that they have."

"Well, Old Blue has been around for as long as I can remember. Anglers have been filling out surveys for the fish and game commission for decades now. Every few years, one fish keeps popping up, getting bigger and bigger."

"Old Blue?" It wasn't really a question.

"Yep. Hard to say exactly how much bigger or if it's still him cause if anyone gets him to take the bait, the line breaks more often than not. Last time anyone had him long enough to weigh in was about five, maybe six years ago. Blue was already at sixty-one pounds."

Logan blew out a sharp whistle.

"That pretty much sums it up." The woman bobbed her head. "Folks figure by now he's got to be close enough to break the state record for largest Striped Bass, maybe even the world record. I suspect that's why the sign up for this tournament is so high even though it's new."

Things were making a lot of sense. Getting up before dawn when the stripers were feeding closer to the surface was something he did often, but he might want to hang out more at dusk now that he knew about Old Blue. Maybe even skip cooking his catch and just turn himself around to search out the deepest hot spot on the lake.

"If you're thinking of heading back out, I wouldn't."

His head snapped around to face her. Was she a mind reader?

"Only time anyone has reeled that fella in has been in the morning. Not much of a night owl apparently."

"I see." He tossed the garlic into a handheld basket and walked over to the small display of produce. It all looked nice and fresh, probably grown in a nearby garden, but his mind kept drifting away to the other night, eating on his porch with Rose. Maybe he should just stick the fish in the fridge and invite her out to dinner.

"You enjoying your stay at Hart Land?"

Granted, they weren't far from the gorgeous old Victorian and the surrounding cottages, but they weren't that far from the Hilltop Inn closer to town either, and as far as he knew, there were smaller inns dotting the area all filled with reservations from fisherman. His thoughts jumped back to what were the odds this woman could read his mind before he decided a lucky guess was more likely. "Yes." More than he'd expected. Maybe dinner out was a bit much and he could invite Rose to join him at the cabin for a fresh fish dinner. He didn't cook like Lucy, but it was hard to ruin grilling fresh bass. Especially with fresh herbs. No. He shook his head. As much as he'd enjoyed their time on the porch the other night, he had to leave her alone. Let her get her work done. Maybe after the tourney. He could stay an extra day or so.

He blew out a soft sigh. Wasn't he presuming a lot. Not only that Rose would be staying on after the tourney, but that she'd want to spend what was left of real down time with him.

"By the way," the angelic woman came around from behind the counter and stuck her hand out, "I'm Katie O'Leary."

"Logan Buchanan," he responded, taking the proffered hand. "A pleasure."

"I have an idea." She spun around and returned to her spot. "I bet if you take this order back to Lucy and mention your catch of the day, she'd probably offer to cook it up for you and," her smile widened, "odds would be even better she'll ask you to join the whole family for dinner."

Okay, that did it. Katie had to be a mind reader. No one was that lucky.

"Here you go." She pushed the box with his purchases forward. "Still want the garlic?"

He glanced down at his basket. Despite walking up and down nearly every corner of the small store, he'd done more thinking about his time with Rose than on cooking supper. Sorry Mom, but looks like being thoughtful is going to take a back seat to any chance of spending a little more time with Rose Preston.

• • • •

Pushing to her feet, Rose twisted left, then right, stood on one foot pulling the other against her rear then did the same with the other, and finally hung her arm over cher shoulder, pulling one elbow close to her ear and then the other. A few seconds of easy stretches every hour or so made her life much less achy. Her sister Violet had taught her that little trick after surviving her first exhibit on the new job.

Somehow she'd managed to turn one portable card table into a mountain of paperwork. She'd spent the better part of yesterday and today on the phone confirming and reconfirming every possible detail. Even the things she wasn't technically responsible for, she followed up with the coordinators to reassure herself. This event meant so much to her grandfather and her cousin Cindy that she wanted to make sure everything went off without a hitch. In a couple of days, the fishermen would be descending on Lawford Mountain like biblical locusts. Some had probably already arrived to scope out the lay of the land.

That brought one tall cowboy to mind. All day yesterday, she'd battled the urge to find any excuse to knock on his door. When dinnertime had rolled around, she'd expected her grandfather to have invited his friend's grandson to dinner with the family, but nope. Then she thought for sure Lucy would fix him a tray like she had the night before, and she'd been ready all through supper to casually volunteer as room service again. Except Lucy hadn't prepared anything for him, and even though the General mentioned inviting him to play cards, he had not joined them for that event either.

Now she considered how awkward would it be if she simply showed up on his doorstep this evening bearing some of Lily's almond cookies that he seemed to like. Or, what if she were to extend an invitation to join the family for dinner. She shook her head. That's all she needed. To alert Lucy's matchmaking instincts, not to mention create fodder for the family and any friends within earshot. The card playing Merry Widows coming to mind. Those ladies gave the old joke telegraph, telephone, and tell a woman new life. No doubt, within hours of inviting him to dinner, the entire town will be privy to the invite, they'd probably have her engaged, married, and pregnant before morning.

About to take her seat and begin going over the checklist in the next section of her binder, the sound of a car door slamming collided with an ear-piercing scream from inside the house. The latter made the hair on the back of her neck stand on end, leaving her no time to contemplate how had she not heard the car drive up to the front of the house in the first place. A second desperate cry of "Lucy" propelled her away from her chair and sent her bolting inside.

The sight of her grandmother standing on a kitchen chair, literally clutching her pearls, and Lucy backed into the corner cabinets jabbing a broom at the countertop brought her to a screeching halt.

"What's the matter?" A deep, now familiar voice floated over her shoulder. Logan must've heard the screams as well. It had probably been his car door that she'd heard slam shut. Rather ironic when you stop to think that daydreaming about him was the whole reason she hadn't heard the car pull up in the first place. Didn't life have an interesting sense of humor?

"Oh, thank God." Grams blew a deep shoulder-relaxing breath and pointed at Lucy.

On the other hand, their normally nonplused housekeeper was still white as a well-bleached sheet and frantically waving the broom around. "I left my phone by the sink," she huffed. "I thought for sure he was going to eat it, or me, before I could call for help." She dared a glance in Rose's direction. "Where the hell did that thing come from?"

Only now did she turn her attention to the sink and take a step back, slamming into the hard chest behind her. "Oh my."

Logan's hands shackled around her arms, holding her steady. "I'd say *Oh my* about covers it." His hands loosened and brushed lightly down her forearms, patting her reassuringly before stepping around her for a better look and slowly inching forward.

She didn't know what had her heart racing faster, the sight of a massive snake curled up in the sink, or the gentle feel of Logan's comforting fingers.

"What are you doing?" Lucy shouted at Logan.

"Getting a closer look." The man had the nerve to chuckle before calmly striding up to the sink, reaching in, and grabbing the slimy thing by either end and lifted what must have been at least four feet of ugly up into the air. "I'd venture a guess that somebody's pet boa constrictor escaped and found its way into your pipes."

Still pointing the broom at him and the snake as if it were a lethal weapon, none of the color had returned to Lucy's face. "Don't those things eat people?"

Logan had the good grace to muffle his amusement. "In order to do that it would have to wrap himself around you and squeeze you to death first. Fortunately, this guy is too little to do that."

Lucy didn't look terribly convinced, but her grandmother seemed a little more reassured. "You're positive he isn't one of those poisonous kinds of snakes?"

"Yes ma'am." He threw her a reassuring smile. "I'm from Texas. Ranch country. I've got a pretty good handle on what's gonna kill my cows or me."

That seemed to be enough for Lucy to lower the broom to the ground and Grams to ease into the nearby chair, both breathing more easily.

"Okay," Lucy said. "Now what do we do with it?"

Rose pulled her phone from her pocket. "I'll call Cindy."

"You can call whoever you want." Lucy waved a finger at Logan and the snake. "But I want that thing out of my kitchen. *Now*."

"I'm afraid I have to agree with her," Grams said.

"If one of you would bring me a pillowcase and a box, we can move him outside until someone more official comes to get him."

"I can handle that." Rose tore off up the stairs and came back with both a pillowcase and one of her file boxes with a lid. For the first time in her life she'd merely dumped the thing on end without any regard to neatness or order and flew back down the stairs. Logan had moved to the back porch and both her grandmother and Lucy looked more like themselves. Especially Lucy, she was already scrubbing that sink within an inch of its life.

"Here you go." She handed him both items. Within minutes, the snake was secure in the pillowcase and resting in the box.

"Just for good measure." He flipped the small café table upside down and set it on top of the box.

Only now did *she* breathe easily. Even though she held every confidence he knew what he was talking about, she was too much of a city girl to take any snake in stride.

"Let's get back inside and check on your grandmother and Lucy." Placing his hand on the small of her back, he nudged her toward the door and once again her heart took off at the speed of a thoroughbred at the derby. Clearly the snake had little to do with her pulse racing.

"You," Lucy whirled around to face Logan, "may have anything you want for breakfast, lunch and dinner for the rest of your stay. I may even consider shipping meals to Texas after you leave if you'd like."

"And I'll see to it that my granddaughter makes your favorite dessert," Grams added. "Do you have one?"

"Maybe something with rum in it," Lucy suggested. "Lord knows about now I could use a shot of my sainted grandmother's peppermint schnapps."

"Right about now I wouldn't object to that either." Grams smiled.

Funny, Rose was thinking she could use a drink too, only something a whole lot cooler. Her gaze drifted to her tall Texan. On second thought, maybe not.

CHAPTER EIGHT

"I bid five." The look of utter and complete frustration on his opponent's face made Logan smile. Normally he wasn't an aggressive bidder in whist, but lady luck seemed terribly enamored with him today.

Chuckling, the General shook his head. "You can play at my table any time you like, young man."

"Back at you, sir." He'd joined the card game over an hour ago and he and the General had won every hand since. If he were a betting man, it would probably have been enough to make him try his luck with the lottery. Though he supposed stumbling into that kind of luck only struck a man once in his lifetime.

"Are you going to stare at those cards all night or are you going to play?" Ralph peered at him from over the rim of his glasses. The man was a natural born storyteller and tonight was no exception. Whether just shooting the breeze or an outright effort to throw him and the General off their stride Logan wasn't sure, but either way, Ralph's impatience was escalating. The interesting neighbor clearly had grown tired of losing.

Logan discarded four cards. "Hearts are trump." From the unsolicited groan that came from Ralph and his partner, the infamous Floyd the barber, Logan was willing to bet he probably should have bid higher than five. If he hadn't been watching Rose from the corner of his eye most of the night, he probably would have better calculated his odds of winning with the hand he'd been dealt and perhaps attempted a six bid. But the truth was that the luck of the cards dealt bolstered by the General's skill had been winning the rounds, not anything Logan was doing. His mind had mostly been on the pretty redhead focusing on the growing mounds of paper in front of her.

The old screen door squeaked open and another redhead carrying a large white box backed onto the porch. "So, who is the conquering hero?"

All the older men at the table glanced up and chorused, "Me."

Shaking her head, the woman marched to the main entryway of the house, pausing at Logan's side. "We haven't met yet. I'm Lily and I have been told that the women in my family are forever in your debt."

"That may be a slight exaggeration." He really didn't get why they were making such a fuss about this. It wasn't like Lucy and Mrs. Hart had found a rattler at their feet.

"When I'm requested to not only bring all the day's leftovers from the bakery but to bring a double chocolate cake, something big is cooking. Or in this case, rescuing. Thank you."

"I didn't do anything anyone else wouldn't have done," he insisted, not that any of the women on the porch were listening.

"That's right." Ralph scowled at the card the General discarded and threw out a lowly two of clubs. "It's times like today that my trusted shillelagh would have come in handy. I'd have clobbered that footless reptile good. He wouldn't be scaring anymore fine ladies to death again."

"Where do you suppose he came from?" Rose lifted her gaze from the paper in her hand.

The General rolled his eyes. "I can't imagine whoever it is will be fessing up any time soon. No one on this mountain wants to scare my sweet Fiona to death."

"What about me?" Lucy came in and set a piece of freshly sliced chocolate cake beside Logan.

"Sorry, Luce." Floyd shook his head. "You may have many a fine quality, but I don't think there is a soul on this mountain thinks of you as sweet."

Lucy didn't bother responding; she merely shot Floyd a sideways glance before rolling her eyes.

"Personally, I think y'all got off easy with the snake," Thelma said from the other table. "Finding a harmless boa—"

"Harmless," Lucy scoffed.

"I'm not saying that in the wild in a jungle somewhere that a full-grown boa wouldn't be a problem. I'm just saying, a trapped raccoon could have been much worse."

"Oh heavens." Mrs. Hart shook her head. "I remember that day. We had the Ladies Art League luncheon here at the house."

Louise, another of the Merry Widows, looked up from her cards. "I wonder if Thelma's little raccoon incident is why we've never done that lunch here again?"

"Little incident?" Thelma glared at Louise. "That animal was trapped in my car for a short while—"

"Not sure he agrees that a five hour luncheon is a short while," Ralph chimed in.

"Whatever!" Thelma waved him off. "The thing defecated all over the car, scratched all the doors, tore up the seats, and if that wasn't enough, peed in the vents."

"It was a bit of a mess," Fiona Hart said sweetly.

"I love you, Fiona, but that has to be the understatement of all time," Thelma said. "I had to buy a gas mask just to clean it out enough and drive it to the body shop. In the end, the insurance company had to total a practically new car."

"New? Wasn't that the Oldsmobile?" Floyd asked.

"It was. Loved that '88."

"They stopped making Oldsmobiles in 2004," Floyd deadpanned.

"Doesn't matter. It was in pristine condition with low mileage and those beautiful Corinthian leather seats." Thelma sighed.

"Those seats were Chrysler," Ralph corrected. "And there's no such thing as Corinthian Leather. It was a marketing ploy that made Chrysler a hell of a lot of money."

"Whatever," Thelma snapped. "The point is it was a beautiful car. Still like new and those blasted raccoons ruined my baby."

"You never did have much luck with cars. Didn't a pack rat nest under your hood?"

Thelma rolled her eyes skyward. "Don't remind me. At least it wasn't a sewer rat or they would have eaten the wires."

"I don't think Jerry at the gas station has ever forgotten opening the hood and all those plastic bags and leaves from the nest falling on his head." Ralph chuckled.

At that exact moment Logan glanced at Rose the same way he'd done over and over this evening, only this time she laughed at the banter and looked up, her gaze meeting his. Her amused grin shifted to a sweet smile and Logan thought he would gladly put up with snakes, raccoons and pack rats if it meant spending more time with Rose Preston.

• • • •

Rose had no idea why she bothered working, she'd lost track of her project at least two hands ago. Instead she was fascinated watching Logan interact with her friends and family. Especially her grandfather. He had just the right mix of familiarity and respect, and she admired that.

"We found the culprit." Cindy emerged from inside the house, a dish of Lily's cake in one hand, a fork in the other, and her sister Poppy and Lily on her heel. "I just got a text from Nadine. She's working dispatch tonight and got a call from city hall. The mayor."

"The mayor?"

Cindy dropped into the seat beside Rose. "The one and only. Apparently her son failed to mention that his pet snake Igor has been missing for two weeks. At first he thought he'd find it somewhere in the house, and then he figured it was gone for good."

"Interesting. The mayor doesn't live that far," Ralph looked up from his cards, "but she doesn't live that close either."

"My guess," the General said, "is he found his way into the sewer line looking for a water source and followed his way into our beloved home."

A bowl of ice cream in her hand, Poppy practically collapsed into the seat on the other side of Rose.

"Another long day?" Rose asked.

"Now half the new moms in the congregation are petitioning the pastor to convince the board to go for the Mother's Day Out program."

"If that many people want it, what's the problem?" Cindy asked.

Poppy swallowed a spoonful of butter pecan. "And there's my problem, because every last one of them has come and sat in front of my desk asking me that exact same question."

"What about the pastor?" Lily dragged the rocker closer to her sisters. "Shouldn't he be fielding his parishioners?"

"He does, but he can only deal with one at a time and you know who gets the overflow."

"It sounds to me like tonight's the night for that wine on the beach." Rose grinned. "Since we couldn't do it a couple of nights ago."

"Do we have the fixings for s'mores?" Poppy asked.

"Have you not ever looked in Lucy's pantry?" Lily rolled her eyes. "That's like asking if the Pope is Catholic."

Poppy burst out laughing. "I know. What was I thinking?"

"Then we're on?" Rose looked from Poppy to Cindy to Lily. All nodded.

"Cole's working tonight so I'm free as the proverbial bird."

"What about Callie?" Poppy asked. "Anyone talk to her today?"

"I think they had practice tonight," Cindy answered. "But I bet she'll stop by afterward. She usually needs adult recharging after spending a few hours with energized teens."

"That she does." Lily nodded. "Besides, who can resist s'mores."

"And wine," three voices echoed, then all four burst into snickering laughs like a gaggle of teenagers keeping secrets from boys.

Speaking of which, Rose looked over to where Logan had tossed down a card and scooped up another trick. He really was on a hot streak.

"I'll call Iris." Poppy reached for her phone.

"I thought she's in New York?" Lily asked.

Poppy sighed and slid the phone back into her pocket. "That's right. They're all visiting Aunt Marissa. I swear, I feel like this week has just been one crazy long day."

"All right." Lily pushed to her feet. "I'll go raid the pantry. One of you hit the wine bar."

"Done." Cindy followed her sister into the house.

"Are you heading home?" Grams asked Poppy.

"Nope." Rose's cousin grinned. "We're heading to the beach."

Grams dipped her chin and nodded. "Someone save me a s'more."

"You should totally join us," her youngest granddaughter said.

"Yes," Rose chimed in. She couldn't remember the last time her grandmother had told them stories of growing up on the mountain and roasting marshmallows by the shore.

Grams shook her head. "Not tonight, girls. But I'll take a rain check. You should invite Mr. Buchanan. I think he's done enough old codger duty. Besides, I think there could be a mutiny if he and your grandfather win another hand." Always looking graceful in her colorful dresses, Rose's grandmother set her pile of braided fabric aside and stood.

It didn't take much convincing from her grandmother for Logan to agree. "May I do anything to help?"

He followed Poppy and Rose into the kitchen after Lily and Cindy. Arms laden with graham crackers, bags of marshmallows, chocolate bars, plates, napkins, skewers, and of course wine and glasses, the five made it halfway to the shore when headlights flickered on them.

"That's either Callie or Alan," Cindy said.

Poppy shielded her eyes toward the house with her free arm. "Unless Alan has grown a ponytail, I think that's Callie."

"Callie it is." Rose waited for her cousin to spot the migrating crowd and waved for her to join them.

"What a great idea!" Callie ran up to the group. "It's been too long since we've done a bonfire."

"Oh, we can do you one better." Rose held a box of graham crackers and Callie's eyes rounded with delight.

Lily chuckled and held up a bottle of red wine. "Nothing goes with chocolate like a good Cab."

"Man," Callie looped her arm around her nearest sister, "I knew there was a reason I love you guys."

Logan muffled a low laugh.

"Something funny, Cowboy?" Rose prodded.

"Since I wasn't blessed with a sister, it's kind of fun to see life wouldn't be very different if I had, except there'd be beer instead of wine, and chips and salsa instead of s'mores. But all in all, there'd still be love and laughter."

"Amen to that." Not many people got the connection the nine cousins shared. Families like hers, and apparently Logan's too, seemed to be growing scarce. Heck, she knew a lot of families where the siblings barely spoke to each other once they left the house, and sadly even a few who had not spoken to each other in years and probably never would.

Through the years, starting the bonfires had been Cindy's job. No one really remembered how she became the designated fire starter, but with an ease that came from years of practice, she had the flames reaching for the sky before Poppy had finished handing out the extra-long skewers the General had made ages ago for nights just like this.

She handed the last one off to Logan. "Here you go."

"Thanks." The Texan stabbed at one marshmallow then another.

"A double sugar rush man," Rose teased.

He dangled the white fluffs over the fire "What can I tell you, I'm a growing boy." Tipping his head to one side, he flashed that winning smile she'd become quite fond of.

"I bet you were a handful growing up." She kept her stick hovering near the fire.

"You know it's going to take all night to toast at that distance." He casually waved his free hand in the direction of her slowly browning treat.

Her gaze shifted to the flames shooting from the middle of the bonfire. "I don't like mine burned."

"Neither do I." He shrugged.

"Then you may have a problem." She pointed to the end of his stick. "Your marshmallows are on fire."

His eyes popped open wide and quickly he pulled the stick out of the flames and blew hard to put out the near raging fire, then turned to face her. Another smile teased one corner of his mouth. "Maybe slow and easy is better."

"Always." She grinned at him. For just a few long moments her cousins' laughter and banter slid away and they were the only two people on the sandy shore. It was a nice feeling.

"Look, shooting star." Poppy waved an arm up to the sky. "'Tis the season."

"Man, that one's bright." Callie lifted her gaze to the heavens. "I love nights like this. Especially this time of year. It's like our own private light show."

"Yeah," Rose added. How long had it been since she'd been so totally and completely relaxed? *Too long.* And how long since she'd enjoyed the company of a nice guy? *Even longer.*

"Wow."

She turned to see Logan leaning back on one elbow, staring up.

"I forget how much the nearby Dallas lights fight the stars."

"That's a shame."

"It is." He continued looking up as if trying to memorize each and every twinkle. "We see more stars than the folks who live in Dallas county proper, but it's nothing like this. And certainly no shooting stars."

"I know. Having people refer to the sky as black velvet makes sense when you're not in Boston."

"Or Dallas."

"Or Dallas," she repeated after him.

"Hey," Callie snapped straight, dragging her gaze back to earth. "Isn't the best night for the annual meteor shower coming up?"

"Night after tomorrow," Cindy answered quickly. "I was thinking about taking Alan up to Eagle Point to watch."

"Oh," Lily rubbed her hands together, "what a great idea."

"You guys do remember," Callie chimed in, "the best viewing is after two in the morning."

"Which is why I'm only thinking about it," Cindy said.

Callie shook her head and sighed. "Not me. I have to deal with a camp full of sugar-rushed teens starting at eight in the morning. I need all the rest I can get before facing them and hanging out on a mountain top at two a.m. isn't going to help any."

"Of course we've had lots of clouds the last few days." Cindy slid her toasted marshmallow between two graham crackers. "If it's a cloudy night it will all be a moot point."

"You forgot the chocolate." Callie pointed to the graham cracker and marshmallow sandwich her cousin was about to bite into.

"I didn't forget. I didn't want any."

"What?" Poppy almost dropped her skewer in the fire. "That's sacrilege not to have chocolate in a s'more."

"So sue me." Cindy licked the oozing marshmallow from the sides of the cracker sandwich and moaned with delight. "Sometimes simple is so good."

"Agreed." Lily bit into her traditional s'more.

Enjoying the easy communing with her cousins, Rose had forgotten all about making her own s'more when a neatly assembled sugar delight appeared in front of her.

"I promise it's not burned." Logan waited for her to accept the offering.

"Thanks." She smiled.

"I was thinking." He stabbed at another marshmallow with his stick and held it to the fire. "This meteor shower."

Thankful for something to do with her hands and a mouth full of s'more to keep her quiet, she merely nodded at him.

"I've heard about this before. Hadn't realized I'd be in the Northeast at the same time. It's supposed to be a pretty spectacular show."

"It is," she concurred, shoving another morsel into her mouth before she said something stupid and romantic too.

"If I stay up to see the show in person, would you care to join me?"

She couldn't have stopped the smile that took over her face even if she'd wanted to. "I'll even bring the blanket."

"Deal." Slowly, he turned his gaze back to the glowing fire.

For the first time in a long time the last thing on Rose's mind was work, to-do lists, and color-coded binders. And maybe that wasn't a bad thing at all.

CHAPTER NINE

Logan had barely crossed over the threshold into Hart House when Lucy grinned up at him. "Breakfast will be ready to serve in just a few."

When he'd agreed to indulge Lucy and let her feed him for the rest of the trip, he hadn't realized that meant from now on he would be imbedded at the Hart family table. Not that it was a bad thing. Especially if it meant spending more time with Rose Preston. Still, a small part of him felt terribly guilty. To him it was akin to taking advantage under false pretenses. The snake really wasn't dangerous, and there wasn't anything brave or heroic about putting the thing in a pillow case to wait for Cindy to come get it.

"The General is already in the dining room. Take a seat and I'll bring in a fresh batch of hot food." Before he could blink, she was off and hurrying into the kitchen.

What he'd really like at the moment was a good, strong, and hot cup of coffee. Not long after they'd begun roasting marshmallows last night, Cindy's fiancé joined the crowd on the beach. The sugar rush had kept everybody talking, laughing, and wide-awake until well after midnight. Callie and Poppy had been the first to leave, blaming early morning work. Cindy, on the other hand, insisted unlike her early-to-rise counterparts, she'd inherited their grandmother Lawford's night owl genes. Shortly after one in the morning, she had stood and announced that night owl or not, she should at least get some sleep before dealing with her patients in the morning. That had left only him and Rose watching the embers blow out and finishing the last drops of wine.

By two o'clock, despite the nonstop conversation covering almost every embarrassing or hilarious moment in their lives from the age of four on, Rose's eyelids were beginning to droop. So much so that she reminded him of his youngest brother, Carson. As a baby, he hadn't wanted to miss anything. Batting eyelashes desperately attempted to remain awake only to succumb to the call of the night. Like Carson, Rose was fighting a losing battle. Despite not wanting their time together to end, he knew with the tournament only a few days away she still had a long to-do list and needed to get at least some sleep, preferably in a comfortable bed. Reluctantly, he'd insisted they call it a night.

"Good morning." Standing by a massive silver coffee urn, Rose appeared a tad too cheerful for someone who'd had as little sleep as he'd had. "Would you like a cup?"

"Yes, thank you."

She handed him two packets of sugar and the steaming mug of hot morning brew she'd just poured. For some reason, that she'd remembered how many sugars he used made his morning feel just a pinch brighter. When she slid the milk decanter in his direction and smiled up at him, the final gesture made his day. Adding a touch of milk to her own freshly filled cup, Rose turned and took a seat at the table. Her animated conversation with the General picked up where it had left off when Logan had entered the room. Clearly unlike Cindy, Rose had inherited the General's early morning genetics.

"And here we go." Lucy strolled into the room carrying a large baking dish and set it on the buffet in front of him. "This is my French toast casserole. I waited for you to arrive. It's best when fresh out of the oven. Enjoy. Eggs will be here in a moment."

He didn't doubt anything that Lucy cooked would be worthy of a five star restaurant. Scooping a spoonful of casserole onto his plate, he added a few strips of bacon from a nearby platter and spun about, almost tripping over one of the dogs. "Well, good morning. Which one are you?"

"That's Sarge," Rose offered.

Setting his plate down, he scratched the dog's ears. "I suppose you want some scraps."

"Nope." The General shook his head. "Not in this house."

Rose rolled her eyes and he shrugged a shoulder at the pup. "Sorry, buddy. You heard the General."

Plate in hand, he took one short step before the second dog trotted up to him.

"Sorry girl, same deal. No food."

The second pup rubbed up against him with such force he had to take a step aside, only to bump into Sarge again.

Rose tapped the seat beside her. "You'd better sit before those two send you flying and waste all that good food."

He'd been thinking the same thing. Not so much about the food flying or the dogs bumping into him, but about taking the empty seat next to Rose.

"Are you enjoying your stay so far?" Mrs. Hart asked.

"Very much so." He'd thought for sure this trip was going to be a bust without his grandfather yet so far it was turning out to be the best vacation he'd had in ages. "Hart Land is a lovely place."

"It is." Fiona Hart nodded. "Not many people see the magic. Too many think only about dollar signs, but Hart Land is special. It's been blessed for generations."

"Hopefully my granddaughters will see to it that this place is a joy for many generations to come." The General stood to refill his coffee. Both dogs had trotted back to their master and remained faithfully at his side.

"I think Poppy is your best bet." Rose looked over to where her grandfather stood by the coffee urn.

The older man didn't say a word in response. He only nodded, filled his cup, then turned back around. "What's on the agenda for today?"

"I have to head over to the Hilltop and start organizing the donations. See if I can get a head start on the layout before the actual start of the tournament keeps me too busy."

"Makes sense." The General took a sip of coffee, and if Logan wasn't mistaken, kept a careful eye on both of them.

What was it his grandfather had called him, Old Eagle Eye? The thought made Logan squirm. What exactly was the General seeing?

"Will you be needing any help?" Mrs. Hart asked.

"Extra hands never hurt."

"Well, I'll be in town today for the Ladies Art League lunch, perhaps I can scrounge up a few sets of helping hands?" The older woman delicately dabbed each corner of her mouth with the white linen napkin from her lap. If ever a person fit the description of a class act, it was Fiona Hart. The woman managed to carry off distinguished elegance blended with colorful artistry. She must have really been something in her younger days.

"Logan," the General addressed him. "You're welcome to join me at the barbershop. There is always an afternoon checkers game, if you have nothing else planned."

Considering he had not played checkers with anyone since he was a little kid, it wasn't a bad offer, but he liked a different idea better. "Sounds good," he said, turning to face Rose. "Unless you can use an extra pair of hands now. I'd be happy to volunteer."

"Oh, I'm sure that would be quite helpful." Fiona swept her glance from Logan to Rose. "Don't you think, dear?"

"I'm afraid it won't be much fun."

Logan chuckled. "I was raised working cattle before the sun rose, this will probably be much more entertaining for me than you think." He didn't want to sound like a sappy greeting card and say that anything that kept him in the same room as her would make his day, but the sentiment was pretty much on target. Who would have ever thought.

• • • •

"I've got several boxes of donations in my room that folks have been dropping off here the last few weeks. That's as good a place as any to start." Rose pushed to her feet. "If you'll follow me, we'll make better time if both of us bring them downstairs."

Already standing, Logan looked to the General and back. "Of course."

Standing in the doorway of her bedroom at Hart House, Rose looked at the boxes to one side. "If you wouldn't mind grabbing the larger one of those, I'll start with the smaller boxes."

"No problem." He stacked half the boxes, did a knee bend and balanced all three as easily as she managed a stack of pillows. A quick trip downstairs and he was back loading the last of the boxes. "Anything else?"

She shook her head and reached for the binder on her desk. Quickly, she stashed a few loose pieces of paper inside and grabbed a legal pad just in case. Both she and Logan took a quick glance around the room. For her, it was much like checking out of a hotel, making sure she had not left anything important behind.

Waiting by the door, Logan's expression softened. "Everything about this house calls for people to come in, put their feet up, sit a spell, and enjoy life."

Rose had to chuckle. "Sit a spell?"

"Hey," he chuckled back, "I am from Texas. At least I didn't say y'all could be fixin' to sit a spell."

"Fixin'?" Shaking her head, she waited until he was in the hallway to pull the door closed behind them. Falling into step behind him, they proceeded down the hall. "Y'all I understand. But fixin'?"

"It's a southern thing. The equivalent of getting ready to."

"I thought as much, but at least y'all comes from you all. That makes sense. Fixing, not so much."

"Then we won't get into figure because southerners do a lot of fixing and figuring."

"You're right." She held back a laugh, surprised at how much she enjoyed the silliest of conversations with Logan. "I'd better quit while I'm ahead."

"Tell me more about the Hilltop?" he asked over his shoulder.

Rose scooted around him and hurried ahead to hold the front door open. "It's the only hotel this side of the lake. The other side is much more commercial and has more lodging accommodations. Most of the fishermen will be staying across the lake."

"But the gala is going to be at the Hilltop?"

"That's right. They have a nice sized banquet facility. The old carriage house, which used to be a stable, was converted into a hall for weddings and other major festivities about five years ago." She popped the hatch of her SUV open.

"And obviously it's worked out?" He deposited the boxes beside the others.

"Totally. Not only do locals need a place for big family weddings, graduations and other celebrations, not all destination weddings are to a beach in the Bahamas. We've all been amazed how many people want a picturesque wonderland wedding and are willing to come from all ends of the earth to do it in these mountains. Seasons don't seem to matter, though January snow and October foliage are pretty popular."

"Makes sense." Logan opened her driver's side door for her. Nothing like a little bit of Texas chivalry. "Texas is both flat and hot. If you want mountains covered in snow, this would do the trick."

"Having lived in places that only had summer three months of the year, I think I'd rather plan a big event locally in warm weather or travel to warm weather. Anyone who has planned anything big in the Northeast in the winter knows nothing can wreak havoc on plans like a sudden snowstorm. Ice covered anything can totally mess up driving, parking, walking, people slipping on the sidewalk, you name it, things happen. If I were planning a winter wedding, it would probably be in the Bahamas."

"So you'd like to get married in the Bahamas?"

Rose pulled onto the main road and wondered how had the conversation taken such an odd turn. "Not really. That was a somewhat convoluted way to say if I ever get married, I would prefer to plan a warm weather wedding. Having grown up on this lake, I don't need to go to the Bahamas for beautiful waterfront."

"I once had a neighbor who grumbled that the manmade lakes scattered across Texas, no matter how big, just wasn't the same as the stream filled lakes from where he grew up. After I few days here I'm starting to agree with him." His gaze drifted out the window into the distance, then turned back to her. "I bet this tournament is going to be a huge success."

"I certainly hope so. We've already sold more tickets to the closing ceremony gala then I had expected. Quite frankly, I've been overwhelmed by the amount of people donating. I thought for sure we were going to have to be begging and pleading people to give. I had nightmares that the silent auction tables would be filled with free haircuts from Betty's Cut and Set, or hammers from Jake's hardware store, and if we were lucky free dinner at Mabel's diner."

"Instead you've gotten 18th century furniture, first edition novels, and many other interesting items."

"Oh yeah." She turned into the Hilltop parking lot. "We even have a week's stay at a castle in Scotland."

"Wow. Who donated that?"

She opened the door and hung one foot out. "You'd be amazed at the friends the General has made through the years. I know I am. At least one of them is a British Earl with a summer home in the highlands."

Circling around to meet her at the back of the car, Logan reached for the boxes. "Looks like I have to remember not to forget my checkbook."

"You might be competing with some heavy hitters. I've made it a point to invite several of the museum's bigger donors." Pulling out the keys that Barb, the owner, had given her, Rose opened the main carriage doors and stepped inside. "You can set those down anywhere."

"Wow." Logan blew out a sharp whistle. "Is all of this for the auction?"

Rose nodded. "Yeah, as the donations came in, Barb has been storing them in the back. She told me last night that they'd brought most of it out here for today to make things a little bit easier."

"Okay, ma'am." He clicked his heels and bowed at the waist. "Where do we start?"

"The idea is to have all the entrants required to file past the auction items in order to register and then again the last night to get to their tables. We'll be setting up as much as we can now. The most valuable items will remain under lock and key in the back until registration starts, but we'll designate an assigned space for it up front."

He nodded.

"The caterers are in charge of setting up the dinner tables and seating the day before the gala." She flipped her wrist to check the time. "I'm expecting some help from Cole and his buddies shortly."

"That's Lily's husband?"

"It is."

They had only set up a few tables when the sound of men's voices rolled into the hall.

"If it isn't my wild Irish Rose," Cole's friend Peyton called out, loud enough to echo through the nearly empty building. "Beautiful as ever."

She knew the bigger than life comment was in fun, but it always made her blush. The little bit of Irish blood that had been passed down from Fiona Lawford's grandmother had given Rose and Lily their red hair and easily flushed complexion.

Logan took a long step closer to her and she turned to make quick introductions. The volunteers sized each other up at a glance. *Men.* Everything was a competition.

"Where shall we get started?" Cole slapped his hands rubbing them together.

Rose pointed to the front. "We set up so that as people arrive they have to pass by the auction items to register then the last night they'll have plenty of time to wander before they find their tables or can get drinks."

"Makes sense." Cole bobbed his head in synchronization with his buddies.

"Going to set most of these on the tabletops by size so that everyone's gaze rises to the larger items in the rear." Rose opened her binder, pulled out one folder spreading out her computerized layout, each table listing items by category size and anticipated value. "I have not had time to label the recent incoming items but anything that matches something on these lists, set it on the appropriate table number and we will sort through as we go."

Logan whistled. "I freely admit, I was impressed with how orderly you managed to maintain your room with your belongings and the auction items, but this is suitable for a military campaign."

"Agreed," Payton said. "Irish, you may have missed your calling. You probably would have made a great general too. Give General Hart a run for his money."

The room filled with loud rumbling male laughter.

Cole shook his head. "Just don't let the General hear you say that!"

"That's all well and good, but let's do some item moving while we're doing all this talking," Rose directed.

"Yes, ma'am." Payton snapped his spine straight and gave a mock salute before turning and lifting the first box.

"I didn't upset you, did I?" Logan asked so close to her ear she could feel the warmth of his breath clear to her toes.

Suddenly all coherent thought seemed to slip away. Somehow she managed to shake her head.

"Good." He smiled on a sigh. "It was meant as a compliment."

Doing her best to channel the confident smile she'd perfected for business, the one that hid all the little girl insecurities that threatened to rear its ugly head whenever something important was at stake, she leveled her gaze with his. "Anything that compares me to either of my grandparents is always a compliment."

"So it should be. You, Rose Preston, are one helluva woman." Still grinning, he turned, lifted the nearest box of donations and walked away as if the deep timber of his voice hadn't just rocked her world.

CHAPTER TEN

"The place looks absolutely fantastic." Logan stood to one side of the door as Rose placed the Hilltop Inn under lock and key.

She slipped the keys into her pocket. "Let's just hope all the attendees are willing to spend a good chunk of their hard earned and won money."

"They won't be able to resist." His stomach rumbled loudly, and for the first time in hours he glanced at his watch. "Wow, I didn't realize how late it is."

"I know I've said it before, but I'm going to say it again, you really didn't have to stay all day."

"It really was my pleasure." He was proud of himself for managing to spit the words out without sounding like a smitten teen falling all over himself declaring *but I really really wanted to.* "What are the odds of my talking you into joining me for dinner?"

Her stomach rumbled. Covering it with one hand, she chuckled. "I'd say the odds are pretty good, but my treat. A thank you for all you've done today."

"That should be the other way around. I should be thanking you for saving my vacation."

"I suppose we could debate this over supper." Her phone rang and slipping it out of her pocket, she looked down and sucked in a sharp breath. "That is if Lucy doesn't kill us for missing dinner at Hart house."

"It is pretty late."

She nodded and swiped her phone, setting it to speaker. "I was just about to call you."

"Sure you were. Fortunately for you, Barb told me that y'all were still working hard at the inn. I'm just checking in to see if you want me to send dinner."

Rose slid into the driver side of the car. "We're both famished. I think we'll just stop at the diner. It's closer."

"You still planning on sitting out on that mountain to stargaze?"

Technically, watching shooting stars did constitute stargazing, but the annual meteor shower that usually graced this part of the country, right in her own backyard, was way more of a light show than mere gazing at twinkling stars. Something she doubted she'd ever grow tired of. "Absolutely. It's been too long."

Lucy chuckled on the other end of the line. "Thought so. I'll have the Star Watcher's Snack ready to go."

"Thanks." A few more words back and forth before Rose disconnected the call and pulled into Mabel's diner.

"Star Watcher's Snack?" he asked.

Shifting the car into park, Rose turned to Logan and didn't bother holding back a smile. "That would be blanket, a variety of cheese, most likely New York Cheddar and gouda since those are Lucy's favorites, pepperoni and salami slices—bite size, of course—apple slices and crackers."

"That's a snack?"

"For Lucy. Yes."

"Does it happen to include a bottle of wine?"

Rose shook her head. "Sparkling water. The General doesn't want anyone either falling asleep on the mountain or driving into a tree in the drunken dark."

"Got it." Logan nodded, holding the diner door open for her. "Sparkling water will be perfect."

"Rose!" Mabel scurried across the floor, skirting past tables filled with patrons. "This is turning out much better than I'd ever expected. I mean, I knew once registration started tomorrow that there was a chance business would pick up, but we've been packed all day already."

The decision had been made for the first year to limit the contestants to only two hundred fisherman. A small part of her had worried how the small town she loved so much would handle the sudden deluge of people, even for only a few days. According to Mabel, so far so good.

"Good to hear. And thank you so much for the trunk. It's a wonderful addition."

"It's for a good cause. Martha is right. It's done nothing but gather dust in the attic for ages." Mabel led the way to the table. "If this is any sign of the next few days, I'm all for doing this every year. Maybe more often. Is it possible to do a tournament twice a year? You know, summer and winter maybe?"

"I don't know." Rose shrugged. She knew art, not fish.

Waving at the last booth in the far back of the building, Mabel stepped aside, grinning like the Cheshire cat. "I just love the sound of a full diner. This is just fabulous."

Rose swallowed hard. A few more days would tell if Mabel was right. Even though she was only technically responsible for the auction portion of the fundraiser, her family had been elbow deep in all the details. She had to keep reminding herself that a fundraiser was a fundraiser and it didn't matter that she didn't do fish. Still, way down she'd been just a pinch on edge. She didn't want to let the family down.

"You okay?" Logan leaned over the table, his voice low and throaty and dripping with concern.

She nodded. "Just thinking."

"That's a new face."

"Excuse me?" As far as she knew she'd had the same face for decades.

He chuckled, that soft smile that made his eyes twinkle. "I've seen you focused—and for the record you look very cute when your brows crinkle together over the bridge of your nose—I've seen you laughing with friends, enjoying family, stressing, relaxing, but this look I don't recognize."

Who was this man that in such a short time he knew her well enough to read the nuances of how she felt? "You recognize my looks?"

"I like faces. Especially," he pressed his lips tightly together before smiling, "yours."

Her heart fluttered and heat filled her cheeks. Not since her freshman year of high school when the captain of the football team had smiled at her one day on the lunch line had she felt so flustered.

"You're worried." It wasn't a question.

"Maybe a little."

"I've watched you. You have all the bases covered. Everything will be fine. No. Better than fine."

That might be true about the tournament, but what about the crazy backflips her heart kept doing every time this man smiled at her?

• • • •

"I bid four," Ralph the neighbor announced, followed by the next player passing and the General giving Ralph what growing up Logan would have called the stink eye. Clearly the former commanding officer had wanted the trick for himself but not enough to bid a five.

For the last few minutes Logan had stood on the old porch waiting for Rose to take a call and watched the card players at different tables. His grandfather had taught him to play whist when he was just a kid. Strategy had been the hardest part when he was young; apparently there was more to it than age because Ralph had clearly misread what kind of hand the General had been dealt. Logan would bet his last dollar that the General's cards very likely didn't mesh at all with Ralph's four bid.

"It's a lovely night for the meteor shower." Fiona Hart glanced up at him from her project in progress. "Some years the clouds don't cooperate, but this year should prove to be one of the spectacular shows."

"Will you be joining us?" He still wasn't sure how many folks would be out for the middle of the night adventure, but it wouldn't surprise him if half the mountain showed up.

Fiona laughed. "Hardly. I may be a night owl by nature but I'm an old owl. I'll be off to bed long before these night owls shuffle their last deck."

"Well," Lucy came to a stop in the doorway, hands fisted on her hips, "got your show time snacks all packed up. Where is Rose?"

"By the car. She got a call from someone named Nadine. Sounds like a guy named Fred went off the wagon."

Rose had covered the cell with her hand and whispered for Logan to wait for her on the porch. The way she'd bit down hard on her back teeth had told him the conversation was going to take more than a minute. He hoped in the end Fred being tipsy would prove more of a nuisance than a real problem, but the ticking clock and the hairs at the back of his neck told him otherwise.

"Oh, that can't be good." Lucy shook her head. "Isn't he one of those people who ride along to keep everyone honest?"

"Yes." The General's brows were buckled together as his gaze shifted from the cards in his hand to the lone figure by her car beyond the front lawn.

From what Lucy had said, it seemed that Fred might be one of the many volunteers Rose had discussed during dinner.

"I told ya that the tourney should be a catch, photo, and release event. Having a monitor in every boat is a royal pain in the astorbar." Ralph rearranged his cards and tossed four aside. "Hearts are trump."

The General didn't utter a word but Logan could almost feel the commanding officer's jaw clench tight enough to crack his molars. The way his gaze bounced back and forth between the cards and the front lawn, Logan wasn't sure if the irritant was hearts for trump or his granddaughter's phone call.

When Ralph led with the ten of hearts and the General played the ace, Logan had his answer. The old guy was unhappy with Rose's call. The screen door squeaked open and Rose crossed the threshold rolling her eyes. "Anyone here care to tell me why Nadine felt I needed to know about Fred?"

"That," the General looked away from the cards on the table, "is what I was thinking."

Rose brushed her hands together and smiled up at Logan. "Well, who does and doesn't ride on the fishing boats when this tournament starts is not on my to-do list."

"No section in that orderly binder?" Logan teased.

Rose grinned up at him. "Absolutely not, which means the only thing I have to deal with now is the light show. Are you ready?"

"And here's your snack basket." Lucy came running out. "Wasn't sure how many folks would show up this year so I packed a little extra."

A little? The basket looked large enough to feed the mountain. "Ready," he answered, taking the basket from Lucy.

"You two enjoy yourselves." Mrs. Hart never lifted her gaze from the strands of fabric draped across her lap.

They'd made it to the car door when he looked back over his shoulder. "What exactly is your grandmother doing?"

"Making rugs," Rose said on a sigh. "I love that woman more than life itself but she is one of the least crafty people I know."

"What do you mean?" He held the door for her.

Rose climbed into the driver seat. "Grams has always been a fan of the arts. It's in her blood."

"And that's how you wound up at an art museum?" Logan kept his gaze on the pretty redhead with such a sweet smile as he fastened his seat belt and Rose pulled out onto the main road.

"Maybe a little, yes. Grams would take us into New York to visit my cousins and the museums and of course, Broadway. When we were old enough she'd take us to some special events and patron parties. MOMA was my favorite. But when an arts and crafts type shopping center opened across the lake, Grams got the bug. She's tried everything under the sun and has yet to find a hobby that suits her."

"That bad?"

"Oh yeah, this latest effort at rag rugs comes from all the leftover fabric from quilting. I'll spare you the rest of the history but at least she keeps trying."

"She'll find something. Persistence is always rewarded eventually. Not always the way you expect, but always in the end."

"That's very profound."

"I don't know about that."

"It sounds like something my grandfather would have said."

"Maybe it's because we both have military grandparents."

"That's right. I'd forgotten." Rose turned up a dirt road. "I checked with Cindy and she wasn't sure she and Alan were going to make it. Something about his muse being on steroids. Apparently he does writing marathons when an idea strikes."

"I see." The General's jeep bounced over a dip and Logan grabbed the hand rail. "Tell me why are we not just watching this from the beach?"

"Great view, but not as great as the top of the world."

By the time they reached the area Rose called Eagle Point, he understood exactly what she meant. Even without looking up, the flashes of light brightened their way. "Wow." It wasn't very eloquent but it fit. "This is amazing."

Rose set the basket down on a log bench then spread the blanket out on a small nearby patch of grass. "It looks like it might be just us."

He certainly wasn't going to complain. Very little held as much appeal as spending time alone with this woman. Not his computers, not his next project, not fishing, not ranching, not even time with his grandfather. Just him, the stars and Rose Preston. Wonder what his grandfather would say about that?

CHAPTER ELEVEN

As a kid, Rose and her cousins had begged to stay up late for the summer shower shows, but not till they were teens did her grandmother pack them up for the nighttime show. She could still remember wishing on all the shooting stars. Silly dreams at the age of twelve. She so badly wanted a *Beauty Light Makeup Mirror*. By fifteen she really wanted Billy Nagle to notice her. In her senior year, admission to at least one of her top three college choices was top of her wish list, and then, well, then life got real and she'd stopped making wishes. Till now. Then again, what were the odds that tonight could go on forever?

"I can't believe this." Head tipped back, sitting with one arm resting on his raised knee, holding a glass of sparkling water, Logan stared upward.

"It is amazing." Setting her paper plate of snacks to one side, she leaned back on her elbows. "I think it beats any Fourth of July fireworks I've ever seen."

"Seriously." He turned to face her and his smile slipped, making his expression unreadable. A slow steady gaze lingered until his lips pressed into a thin line and he turned back to the skies.

Silence hung for a few seconds. The mood had shifted. The light banter had taken a back seat to something new. What she didn't know was if that was good or bad, or if it had anything to do with her or everything to do with the overwhelming natural beauty of a night like this.

"It's like someone took a paint brush and just started streaking sparkle paint across the night."

"Yep." She chuckled, relieved to be back to simple conversation and just enjoying the night. "That about covers it."

"Though this spot seems pretty spectacular even without the magnificent light show. Reminds me of the quiet of the ranch, and that I really need to take more time to slow the heck down. The business world makes it too easy to get wrapped up in the rat race." Shifting his weight toward her, he faced the log bench beside them. "This piece looks to have a lot of history."

"It does." She sat up again and filled her water glass. "It's been in the family for generations. All the Hart couples have carved their initials in it."

"All?" He brushed his hand gently across a section of rough, uncarved bark.

"Yep. Including Lily and Cole and Iris and Eric." She explained the history of the first Hart to carve the log bench for the woman he loved. "We know there's no such thing as a lucky charm, but we all feel as though adding our names to the log gives us a leg up. Sort of a blessing for a long life together." She shook her head. "I know it sounds silly."

"No. It sounds kind of...sweet." He smiled down at her. "A beautiful story. Romantic."

"I always thought so but didn't think most men would agree."

Logan shrugged. "I agree."

"Yes, but if I've learned anything about you the last few days, it's that you don't seem like most men."

He stared at her a moment. "I hope that's a good thing."

Her heart did a little jig. It was one thing for her to slowly discover this guy was polite, and thoughtful, and nice, and, well, not a jerk, but knowing he wanted her to think good of him, that it mattered to him, that made her want to twirl on the mountaintop like a sappy old romance movie. And wasn't that just ridiculous. "It is."

Fingers weaved behind his head, Logan laid fully back on the blanket, looking up. "Sounds like there are a lot of romantics on this mountain."

"What do you mean?" Had she given away the questions rattling around in the back of her thoughts? Surely the guy couldn't read minds.

"Didn't you say that Lucy considers herself the Dolly Levy of the mountain?"

Lucy? Rose shot straight up and stared down over him. "I love Lucy to death, but no, her antics are not romantic. The woman might be a romantic at heart, but it's kind of like Lucy Ricardo wanting to sing on the *I Love Lucy* show. No matter how often she tried she still sounded like nails on a chalkboard. A singer she would never be. Our Lucy's antics are not romantic."

"Did you know in real life Lucille Ball could carry a nice tune?"

"No, but that doesn't make Lucy locking two people in a shed romantic, or setting two strangers on a wild goose chase with no gas in the tank, or *accidentally* forgetting to open the flue and start a fire so the firemen would come running—"

"You're kidding me? That sweet lady?" Logan cut her off, biting back a laugh.

"Nope." She folded her arms across her chest, shaking her head. "Want to hear that *sweet* lady's latest?"

"I'm not so sure, but I'm a big boy. Go for it."

"The church where Poppy works got a new piano player a few months ago. The woman moved here from South Carolina. I never got the chance to meet her, but I heard she was a bit shy and kept to herself and very faithful. Volunteered with Wednesday night bible study. What most folks would probably describe as a good, God-fearing woman. So of course, Lucy thought it would be nice if this good woman met some of Lawford's more eligible good men."

"That seems reasonable," Logan ventured.

"So does pouring gasoline on fire ants if you're not worried about poisoning the water table." She waved her hand at him. "Anyhow, Lucy is very fond of the pastor. Honestly, I can't blame her. I've met him a couple of times and he's a very nice guy who happens to be good looking, and because he's single, he's the target of just about all the matchmakers in town, including the Merry Widows."

"Merry Widows?"

"Long story and this little tale is already long enough, but just so you know Thelma and Louise from the card games are members. So is Nadine Baker. Anyhow—"

"I probably don't want to question the Thelma and Louise thing, do I?"

She merely shook her head and kept talking. "On the surface the nice, old-fashioned, God-fearing southern girl and country pastor seem like a good fit."

Logan nodded.

"Any normal person might have thrown a dinner party for the two to have a chance to socialize outside of church business, or maybe an afternoon barbecue. Something casual and non-committal."

Again, he nodded at her.

"George the Hart Land handyman had two tickets to see a popular comedian playing in a little club in the next bigger city. Since last minute he decided to go out of town that weekend to visit family, Lucy asked if she could have them."

"I detect a plan forming."

Rose bobbed her head. "Yep. She gave the pastor the tickets in front of the new piano player and suggested they should go together. Thanks to Lucy, awkward moment number two hundred and twenty. Neither could get out of it without offending Lucy or each other."

Logan lifted a brow at her.

"Yeah, you see where I'm going with this?"

"Dare I ask who the comedian was?"

"I forget his name, but do you remember Sam Kinison?"

"Yes. He made his career by screaming his comedy. Much of it punctuated by four letter words."

"That's the guy. Compared to the comedian Lucy sent the pastor to see, Sam was a choir boy."

"Ouch." Logan's face contorted in empathetic pain.

"The nice southern piano player has since moved back to South Carolina."

"I think I'm getting the drift, but I don't discard that Lucy isn't a romantic, just misdirected."

"And we all pray we don't wind up in her sights."

"She did pack us a nice picnic basket. Most people would consider this fruit and cheese spread on a blanket under the stars very romantic."

"Trust me, if romance was Lucy's intention all hell would be breaking loose."

"I don't know that even Lucy could muck up a night like this." He lifted his gaze to the stars then back to her. "Everything is perfect."

She certainly couldn't argue that. The stars were putting on a light show as spectacular and awesome as she remembered, and she was sharing it with the nicest guy she'd met in a very long time. Maybe ever? How sad was that? Either she'd spent way too much time building a career or all the nice guys had fallen off the face of the earth. Maybe just a little of both.

"You look suddenly serious." Lost in her own thoughts, she hadn't noticed Logan leaning up on one elbow again and staring down at her. The bridge of his nose creased with concern. "Please don't tell me you're thinking about the tournament."

"No. Not at all." Even in the pitch black of night, backlit with the show above, she could clearly see the intensity in his gaze.

"Good." He leaned slightly forward. "I feel like the geeky kid out with the prom queen."

"Excuse me?"

"Even sopping wet and caught—literally—off guard, that first day only a blind man could have missed how beautiful you are."

"Oh." She should probably say something like thank you, but her mind could only circle around the sincerity in his tone. He liked her. Really liked her.

"Ever since we set up here, I've been dying to do something."

"Oh?" Great vocabulary Ms. Suma Cum Laude. "You have?"

"This." Gently pressing against her, his lips barely descended on hers.

The jolt struck her all the way to her toes. Tender, gentle, soft and tingly, the sweet sensation sent all thought scrambling. Now more than ever she really wished time would just stand still. Star light, star bright...

• • • •

Not only had Rose not slapped him upside the head, she'd kissed him back. Really kissed him. The moment her fingers slid up his arms and reached across the back of his neck, the feeling of coming home settled in hard and strong. Right alongside the yearning for so much more than a single kiss on a mountain top in New England.

The need to pull her impossibly closer and keep her there warred with the small threads of sanity that shouted for him to pull away, to apologize, to excuse himself and take a nice very long, very cold shower. His fingers tangled in her hair—soft and silky—and the voice of sanity gave one more shout, urging him to pull back, to take a long deep breath. Slowly, he eased his head away, shifting his weight.

Rose's eyes fluttered open. Under the flashes of bright lights, pools of deep green locked intently on his. Slowly the corners of her lips tilted upward in the tiniest of smiles. "That was nice."

More than nice. "Very."

"I don't suppose you want to do it again?"

Boy did he. Letting his head tip back momentarily, he sucked in a long, hard breath. Without saying a word, a hand on either side of her, he leaned in for one more kiss. Just one, he told himself. They'd come to this spot for the meteor show, not to make out like a couple of hormonal teens in the backseat of their parents' car. Except no matter how loudly the small voice in the back of his mind reminded him, he couldn't make himself end the kiss. Not until instincts from years on the range working the land and noticing the smallest change in their surroundings reared its head at the sound of crunching underbrush growing louder. Easing up and focusing in the direction of the sounds, he lowered his voice. "What kind of animals do you have up here?"

"That's a pretty long list." She'd already shifted around him and sat up, looking in the same direction he was. "Most of them should be much smaller than either of us."

Dipping his chin, he slanted a glance in her direction. Nothing about those last words made him feel better about being alone on the mountain with a beautiful woman who he liked way more than he should after only knowing her a few days, and not a weapon in sight. Pushing to his feet, he extended his arm and pulled her to stand beside him, ready to move her behind him if whatever was making so much noise proved to be a problem.

A spot of light shone in the distance. Not the flash of the shower above, but a wobbly light that he doubted seriously had anything to do with a vicious and hungry wild animal and everything to with the upright human kind.

"Hi there."

Two shadows emerged from the edge of the path they'd ascended earlier and Logan looped a hand around Rose's waist and shoved her a little harder than he should have behind him.

"Lily?" Rose's voice questioned from behind him.

"Hey. Can't a girl change her mind?" Lily appeared in the reflection of the flashlight held by her husband, and huffing lightly, came to a stop in front of them. "Actually, I woke up way before my alarm."

"And I couldn't fall asleep." Cole turned off the flashlight.

"So, since we were both awake at this inhuman hour of the night…"

"You decided to come watch the stars," Rose finished for her.

Lily nodded. "And I'm hungry. Any food left?"

"Lucy packed enough for half the town." Rose pointed to the basket.

Following the direction of his cousin-in-law's finger, Cole shifted his gaze from the basket of food to the blanket on the ground and then up to Logan. "Sorry if we interrupted anything."

"Not at all," Rose said quickly.

Logan merely shook his head. He had no business letting his mind wander places it had no business going. Not with someone as special as Rose.

"I'm almost surprised to see you still here." Lily rolled a small blanket out beside the one Logan and Rose had been on. "With the tournament registration starting in the morning and all."

Logan hadn't given that the slightest thought. Tomorrow—make that today—at nine am the registration desk at the Inn would open. Fisherman would be arriving in droves to register early before the start of the tourney the next day. If she was going to be hovering over that the way he suspected, she was going to need a good night's rest. And considering the hour already, that didn't seem terribly likely. He could almost hear his mother shaking her head at him. He should have been more thoughtful of Rose. Then again, maybe his real problem was thinking of Rose a little too much.

CHAPTER TWELVE

"Everything all right, dear?" Fiona Hart looked over her shoulder at her husband. Sitting in his favorite chair, a dog at either side, the man she loved may have been gazing out the window, but his thoughts were a million miles away.

"They seem happy, don't you think?" Intent on a distant point, the General's gaze never faltered.

Fiona glanced out the window in the direction of her husband's attention. Yesterday's registration for the fundraising tournament had gone off without a hitch. By mid-day things had been running so smoothly her granddaughter Rose had come home and managed to sneak in a short nap.

Now, even though the sun was nowhere to be found yet this morning, Callie, Poppy, Cindy, and Iris were scurrying about like ants. Carrying things from the house to Rose's car or setting up the weigh in tent on the Point. Whatever was needed, the work was being done without question and with a smile. For the most part. Fiona's grandchildren made her proud. Each one pitching in where they could. Even at this unholy hour of the morning. Cindy's fiancé and Iris' husband appeared to have been designated to do the heavy lifting. From the smile on the men's faces, neither seemed to mind. "That they do," she agreed.

A lifetime ago Fiona had learned to rise with the sun in order to enjoy the morning with her husband. Having him at her side each and every morning since his retirement was something she'd waited a lifetime for. She cherished every moment together. Especially when she thought of how different their lives could have been. So many women kissed their husbands goodbye, sent them off with Uncle Sam to parts of the world unknown, and never had the pleasure of sharing another breakfast.

"Seems like yesterday, doesn't it?" The General had become more nostalgic over the last few months. Always a gun ho Marine looking to the future, despite their advanced years. Until that grim day. Now he looked to the past a tad more often than before he was forced to stare down fate.

She couldn't blame him. The bitter aftertaste of her own fear continued to linger in her mouth.

"Don't you go there." Hand extended, Harold Hart looked up at his wife and smiled. "The next generation is finally getting it right. Soon we'll enjoy another lifetime together with great-grandchildren filling this old place with laughter."

"And chaos, no doubt."

"No doubt." He chuckled.

Fiona squeezed his hand and leaned against him. "I think I'm going to like that."

• • • •

So far, so good. Rose looked around the Point. Plenty of room for fishermen to check in. The tables and scales were all in place. All the volunteers had arrived on time for their assigned tasks. Weigh in wouldn't start till four o'clock this afternoon. She glanced at her wrist watch. If she hurried, she could have one semi-relaxing cup of coffee with her grandfather before the bustle of the day took over.

"Looks good." The General's familiar voice sounded behind her. As usual, Lady and Sarge at his side. "I hear there were some last minute registrants last night."

"Quite a few." She was more than delighted she wasn't in charge of that aspect of the tournament. Last night, watching the volunteers check off lists, compare driver's licenses and IDs, and hand out badges almost had her breaking out in a rash. As it was, she had her hands full with the door prizes. Praise the heavens she came from a big family and that Cindy and Callie were very possibly more organized than she was. She couldn't imagine getting through everybody tugging at her at once without them.

"What now?" he asked.

"Now," she smiled up at him, "I sneak back to the house for a cup of coffee and maybe one of Lily's leftover muffins." Anyone who had ever tasted one of her cousin's muffins would agree that even day old was often better than most people's fresh baked.

"Smart girl."

"Sorry I took so long." Fiona Hart waltzed up to them. "One of the guests in the Elm cottage needed fresh towels, and I told Lucy I'd handle it since George is volunteering with the fishermen."

"Shall we?" The General extended his elbow and in an often practiced motion, her grandmother's hand slid comfortably home.

Taking a moment, she watched her grandparents stroll away along the water's edge. Rose loved the way her grandparents still lit up like besotted teens in each other's company. Sometimes she wondered if she would ever get so lucky in life or if the days of loyalty, devotion, and old fashioned romance were simply long gone. Then she'd look at some of her cousins and think maybe this generation still stood a chance.

She'd barely crossed into the foyer when Logan exited the dining room, a travel coffee mug in each hand. "Oh, good morning."

Damn if that man's smile didn't make all coherent thought slip out her ears. "Morning."

"I figured you might be too busy to come in. I was going to bring you this." He shot his arm out at her, dangling the bigger cup. "Milk, no sugar."

Maybe it was silly, but the idea that he'd noticed how she liked her coffee *and* remembered *and* thought enough to bring her a cup made her downright giddy. "Thank you, but I expected you to be on the lake battling the crowd for a spot."

"Ah, you see," his brows lifted and dropped, making his eyes twinkle, "I have a plan."

"You do?" Dipping her chin slightly, she blew on her coffee but kept her eyes level with his.

He took a slow swallow of his morning brew. "I've already scoped out where the fish like to hang out, and determined they're not early risers."

"You're kidding?"

"Nope." He shook his head. "Usually fish like the early morning dark."

"Which is why fishermen have been out there for hours."

He nodded. "And normally I'd be out there with them, but every time I've been out the last few days, the fish haven't taken the bait, so I didn't see any reason not to enjoy Lucy's breakfast this morning."

Like she'd said all along during the planning and executing of this little venture, she knew art, not fish. "If you say so."

"I do. Do you have time to get something to eat? There's still quite a spread in the dining room."

"Actually, I was just on my way to grab a muffin. I don't like to eat a heavy meal on a busy day. Just slows me down."

"Then you're in luck. Lucy said something about Iris dropping off more muffins and croissants than she knew what to do with."

Rose couldn't stop the tiny moan of delight that escaped her lips. Like it or not, Rose was willing to take odds that she was about to have a big and heavy breakfast.

"The wheels are turning."

"Excuse me?"

"You're thinking about something. My guess is it's more of a debate."

"You might say that."

His gaze lingered and after a few seconds reading her as if she were a paperback novel, he nodded. "Not fish and art. You're thinking about Lily's food."

She tapped the tip of her nose with her finger. "Bingo. Give the man a prize." Immediately she shook her head and waved her hand. "Nix that. I don't want to think about prizes until I have no choice later this afternoon."

"It wasn't that bad."

"No. I suppose not, but I appreciated everyone's help. I know I said it before, but I'll say it again. It was very nice of you to jump in and help last night."

"You're welcome." He turned a few degrees and tipped his head toward the food in invitation, then followed her into the dining room. "What time are you on duty?"

"Not till weigh in."

"Really?" He held the door open for her.

"Really." She smiled up at him and hoped she didn't look like a smitten high schooler crushing on the new teacher.

"I don't suppose," he set his mug on the table and pulled a chair out for her, "you'd like to join me this morning?"

"Aren't you fishing?"

He nodded.

"Oh." Sometimes she was a little slow on the uptake. "You want me to go fishing with you?"

Again he bobbed his head. "Give me a chance to show you the fun side."

"Fun?" She glanced up at him without lifting her head higher. "With fish?"

A loud rumble of laughter sounded. "Yes, with fish." A curtain seemed to drop, hiding all expression. "And me."

• • • •

He was completely sure she was going to turn him down flat. She'd made it quite clear that first day on the water that she would stay away from boats and fishing for perpetuity. It was rather smug of him to think she'd make an exception for him. Even if she did seem to like kissing him.

When she nodded and told him to wait while she changed clothes, he wasn't sure who was more surprised at her response—him or her—because frankly she seemed just as startled as him to hear the words slip from her lips.

Less than an hour later and here they were pulling quietly into Morton's Cove. From the way her eyes circled round like a startled owl, he was pretty sure she recognized it.

"You like to live dangerously, don't you?" It wasn't really a question.

Which was a good thing because he didn't have an answer for her. He held out his phone and kept his eyes on the screen. "Turns out this is the best spot on the lake for actually catching fish."

Rose stretched her neck to see. "Dare I ask what you're doing?"

"Locating fish." Slathered in triple digit sunscreen, covered from head to toe and wearing a hat that was almost bigger than she was, the woman was absolutely adorable and totally irresistible. Keeping his eyes on the fish was his best defense.

"Really?"

"Mm hm." He glanced up at her. "Competitive anglers have all sorts of tricks to help them find where the fish are, how deep they are, you'd be amazed."

"I already am. Still I can't imagine that very many back-to-nature, up to their hip boots in water fishermen are using modern technology as easily as you do."

"It's not that hard."

"Not for a geek. Is that legal?" Her tone was only half kidding.

Determining this was as good a place as any to drop his line, he set down his phone and glanced up at her. "In the rule book."

"That would be the one I told Nadine I'd read when I volunteered to monitor your honesty instead of Bobby from the marina."

"That would be the one." He smiled. From what he'd overheard of her conversation this morning, he was pretty sure she had no idea what the rules were or what she was committing to. Fortunately for everyone involved, he wasn't nearly as competitive as some anglers, not at all ruthless, and the truth was that this had been more about an opportunity to spend time with his grandfather than win the coveted prize money. Or in the case as it be now—spend time with Rose.

"So. Now what?" she asked.

"That depends. Are you going to simply monitor, or do you want to try to catch a fish or two? Of course you're not registered for the tournament, so your catch won't count for anything, but…"

"It's supposed to be fun."

Maybe fun wasn't quite the right word. "It's relaxing. I suppose the best part is communing with nature."

The pointed glare she cast in his direction had him fighting back a chuckle. "Okay, maybe not communing with nature so much as sharing quality time with people you like."

"That I can buy." Her gaze shifted to the gear and tackle in the boat. "Since I can't possibly reel you in again, I might as well give it another shot."

"Works for me." He leaned forward to grab an extra pole when her fingers gripped his forearm.

"But wait. The winners are based on total fish weight, not just fish count. What if I catch a bigger fish than you? I could be stealing an opportunity for you to have a higher weigh in."

The deep concern in her eyes reeled him in as easily and surely as she'd done with the fishing rod not all that long ago. "I don't think you have to worry about that. It's a big lake. There are a lot of fish. *Que sera sera,* so to speak."

Rose shook her head and smiled. "I think we'd be better off if I just cheered you on. After all, with my record, who knows what I'd catch."

That made him laugh. "Not that I'm saying I agree with you, but okay."

Within minutes he'd caught his first fish. Working the reel, it took a little bit to bring the guy in. "I'm guessing this guy's going to be about five pounds, maybe six."

"How can you tell?"

"He's putting up too much of a fight to be a little two or three pounder." Once the fish was on the boat he removed the hook and used another app to do an unofficial weigh of the fish.

Brows crinkling, Rose pointed at the fish. "Do you have an app for everything?"

"Pretty much." He smiled and returned his attention to the weight. "Yep. Five and a half pounds. Looks like it's going to be a good day."

"Now what?"

"He goes in here." Logan placed the fish in the living well. Since this was a catch and release tournament and they weren't keeping track of their own weigh-ins, the fishermen were to keep the fish alive until the official weigh in at 4 PM. "How well we keep the fish until the weigh-in is part of the scoring."

Rose nodded. "I guess I really should read rules."

"How were you to know you were going to tag along today instead of a tournament official?"

"True." She rubbed her hands together enthusiastically. "You know, this competition thing is kind of exciting. I wonder how long before you get another nibble."

He shrugged. "We'll have to wait and see."

Over the next couple of hours he got way more fish than he'd expected, almost all of them five or six pounds. He caught an eight pounder and a couple of fish too small to keep that he immediately threw back. They nibbled another delicious snack packed by Lucy, cook extraordinaire. The woman may be a lousy matchmaker according to Rose and her family, but she knew how to pack a snack basket like nobody's business.

"Are there any more of those little breakfast quiches?" he asked, holding his rod steady and staring at the still waters. A small part of him wondered if it might not be time to shift to another spot. Like people, fish didn't stay in one place for long.

Rose ruffled through the small cooler. "No quiche but she gave us some almond cookies."

"The crescent ones Lily makes?"

"Those would be the ones." Rose smiled. "Lucy is a fantastic cook, but with a few exceptions she leaves all the baking to Lily."

Something tugged on his line. "Looks like we've got another one." Once again like the one just before, he and the fish did battle. "Boy, this guy's putting up a fight. I think he might be the biggest one yet."

Rose slapped her hands together in excitement. "You don't think it's Old Blue, do you?"

"I doubt it." He shook his head, determined not to lose this guy. "This fish is putting up a fight but nothing like I'd have with a fish as big as Old Blue."

Finally, he won. Reeling in the line, the fish broke the surface, rising up before him.

"Oh my gosh," Rose exclaimed.

A satisfied grin tugged at his cheeks. "I know. This guy's got to be at least ten pounds."

"No," she said more forcefully. "That."

Before Logan could follow the direction she pointed at or finish reeling in his catch, wings spread wide, an eagle swooped down low, snatched the fish with his claws, and without slowing down, soared to the sky again. "Oh, hell."

"Wow."

He turned to face her. Wide, beautiful green eyes filled with awe, coupled with a kissable mouth hanging slightly open, and suddenly he didn't care so much that the eagle had stolen his best catch of the day. As a matter of fact, if it would give Rose that much pleasure, he'd gladly let every bird on the mountain steal all his fish.

CHAPTER THIRTEEN

Feeling, as her Grams would say, dead and too dumb to fall over, Rose sank into the porch rocker and debated how badly she wanted to put her feet up. The nearest ottoman was across the porch. It didn't take long for keeping her feet on the floor rather than fetching the ottoman to win her mind's inner battle. "I feel like that was the longest two hours of my life."

"Why is that, dear?" Grams didn't bother looking at her granddaughter. Fiona Hart had progressed from braiding fabric scraps to tying the long strands together in a circle. Every time the beloved grandmother looked up, something would go wrong. As a result, Rose and her cousins had quickly grown accustomed to conversing with the top of their grandmother's head.

"Two hours weighing fish after fish after fish. And some of those men, jeez." Rose sighed. "You'd think a tenth of a pound were a matter of life and death."

"You know how men and their hobbies are." Grams continued to wield the longest needle Rose had ever seen.

With her Grams' track record, Rose was actually afraid the woman might sew herself to the rug.

"I do believe it brings out the conquering spirit as much as a football championship. Friday night lights are nothing compared to a man and his fishing prowess."

Rose hadn't thought her grandmother knew anything about football and Friday night lights. Then again, Fiona Hart had always been a marvel, why should this subject be any different. *Speaking of prowess.* "How's the rug coming?"

"I'm not sure why, maybe it's the size of the needle, but sewing this seems less challenging than quilting."

"The needle is easier to see." And, Rose would think, easier to sew yourself to something, but what did she know.

"It certainly is a world easier than those nasty lures."

"Lures?"

"Yes. Years ago. For your grandfather." Fiona frowned, stabbing more forcefully at a swath of fabric.

Somehow, Rose was fairly positive she was missing something. "Lures for the General?"

"They were always so pretty. I thought it would be fun to make him a few for his birthday. Men seemed to treasure their favorite lures."

Fishing. They were still talking fishing. While the conversation made more sense, the thought of her grandmother and sharp objects like hooks and needles made Rose's blood run cold.

"A few turned out rather nicely, I thought. Did you know fish love shiny things?"

Rose shook her head. The day she'd gone fishing with her grandfather he'd used live bait. The memory of the squirmy little critters was enough to give her the heebie-jeebies.

"Anything really. Bottle caps, beads, coins. Of course we'd have to tie them to something with wire. Corks were my favorite. Easy on the hands." Fiona paused and glanced up. "Loved working with the beads and feathers."

Feathers? Feathers weren't shiny. Maybe Rose needed a footrest and a drink. Then it wouldn't matter what fish liked.

"But for some reason your grandfather switched to live bait and I had no reason to work with the lures anymore." Grams returned her attention to the rug, a frown deepening between her brows.

Rose didn't dare ask what had gone wrong with this project to cause the sour expression.

"Uh oh." Lucy stepped onto the porch. "Is that rain?"

Rose opened her eyes. Darn, it was.

Fiona glanced outside. "Forecaster on the news said it's going to lighten up before morning."

"I certainly hope so." Rose sighed.

"I'm sure it will be fine. At least it's not very heavy." A glass of lemonade in each hand, Lucy handed one to Rose. "What time do you have to be at the Inn?"

"Thanks. And I don't." By the end of last night, they'd worked out a system so close to foolproof that anyone could make sense of it.

Fortunately, she didn't have to worry about just anyone. Since both Cindy and Lily worked in town, they would take care of dispersing the day's door prizes—she flipped her wrist and glanced at the time—as of ten minutes ago. If she didn't hear from her cousins in the next few minutes, she would assume all was well. Tomorrow would be the big day. Last day registrants, another day of fishing, weighing, and hopefully limited mediation, all culminating with a banquet, awards, and the auction. Yep, she was going to have her hands full. She'd kill to have her assistant at her side now.

The family's longtime housekeeper didn't utter a word. One eyebrow arched higher than the other spoke volumes. She thought Rose should be there.

"Cindy and Lily are handling it," Rose explained. "There aren't as many to disperse as last night so it should be easy work for them."

"If you say so." Lucy shrugged and handed the other lemonade to Grams. "As long as you're here, supper will be served in about twenty minutes."

Supper. Rose resisted the urge to glance in the direction of Logan's cabin.

"Thank you, Lucy. This always hits the spot." Grams took a long swallow and then held up her handy work. Rose had a feeling there weren't supposed to be quite so many gaps, but for a first attempt it wasn't half bad. Maybe Grams had finally found her talent.

"It's better," Lucy said softly.

Better?

"We might be able to use this one," Grams responded.

"This one?" Rose voiced out loud. "How many do you have?"

"This makes four," Grams offered.

Oh, dear. Rose had a feeling rag rugs would soon be a thing of her grandmother's past, no matter how much fabric she had stashed in her craft room. And paints. And yarn. Oh, did the woman have an eternal supply of yarn. Even after she'd stopped knitting or crocheting, Grams and the General would make a monthly trek to the specialty shop outside Boston. From the glimpse Rose had gotten earlier in the week of the storage closet, Grams clearly couldn't resist the stuff, and Rose suspected soon the family would be up to their eyeballs in yarn snowballs. Though now that she thought about it, no one had mentioned the specialty shop for some time. Maybe her grandmother had finally lost the penchant for yarn shopping.

Speaking of penchants, the porch door squeaked, inching open, and tall, dark and Texan walked onto the porch. Just her luck, a man finally makes her heart dance by merely breathing, whose company she actually enjoyed, and he had to live halfway across the country. What was the saying: all good things must come to an end. *Too bad.*

"Evening," Logan directed to everyone within earshot.

"How did you do?" Lucy asked.

"They don't have the tallies posted yet, but I had the most weight of the handful of guys I could hear who went before me."

"Ooh. Isn't that nice." Grams continued her efforts with the rug.

Rose nodded and Lucy scurried away, calling over her shoulder, "I'll bring you some lemonade. Fresh squeezed too."

"That woman is spoiling me." Logan straddled the chair closest to Rose. "Do you think if I proposed she'd be willing to move to Texas?"

Chuckling, Rose did her best to keep a straight face. "It won't be her first."

"Now why doesn't that surprise me?" Logan smiled. "Looks like you're stuck with me."

Stuck with him. Why did that not sound a bad thing at all?

● ● ● ●

Only a week ago Logan was dreading being stuck here at the lake on his own and now he couldn't think of any place he'd rather be.

"I guess with the tournament, the evening card game is on hold?"

"Maybe, maybe not. You never know who's going to show up." Fiona Hart put her project aside and craned her neck to look into the foyer.

"So tell me, Logan." Fiona Hart smiled up without raising her head. "Did you catch Old Blue?"

He shook his head. "Though I heard someone named Ned claims to have hooked him and then he broke loose."

"Pish posh," Fiona sputtered. "That man's fish stories are as long as his boat."

"I'm kind of glad no one caught him." Rose leaned back. "Even if it was a catch and release tournament, I'd hate for something to happen to him. He's such a legend around here."

"I suppose you're right." Fiona paused her work and glanced toward the doorway. "I do believe your grandfather has lost track of time. That computer can be intoxicating."

"Cell phones too," Rose added. "There are days I wonder why the heck people pay to come to an art museum if they don't lift their noses out of their phones."

He certainly wouldn't disagree, though in his case that cell phone addiction had proved quite lucrative and he'd liked to think he'd learned a little something about putting his techno gadgets away and just enjoying the world around him.

Footsteps accompanied by four-footed paws clacking on hardwood drifted onto the porch, bringing a smile to his hostess' face. "There you are, dear."

"Was just on the phone with Ralph. He's going to stay in town this evening. Going to dinner with Ned and Nadine." The General turned to Logan. "And I understand congratulations are in order."

"Sir?"

"You're in the top five."

"Oh, isn't that lovely," Fiona Hart cooed, once again returning to work on her rug.

"How do you know?" Rose frowned at her grandfather. "The official tallies aren't supposed to be posted until later tonight."

General Hart made little effort to smother his amusement. "Rose, every member of the tournament committee is one of my dearest friends."

"And blabbermouths," she huffed before smiling. "Congratulations."

"Thanks, the scales were good to me. Which reminds me." Logan retrieved the paper he'd carried all afternoon from his breast pocket, laid it on the table in front of the General, and carefully unfolded it. "This was on a fish I caught today. I don't know how we missed it, but the scale guy noticed it when they were weighing my catch."

"That was *on* a fish?"

"Yes, sir."

"Not in it?"

"No, sir. It was hooked deep in the fish's tail. Looks like it's been there a good long time. A few of the men figured maybe the fish shook it loose from his mouth and it slipped to his tail."

Rose reached out and lifted the bead clad lure. "Oh, how pretty. This is rather unusual, isn't it?"

Glancing up from her project, Fiona Hart's eyes circled round. "Oh, my." Stabbing the needle into the rag strip, she reached forward slowly and lifted the lure to the light. "Aunt Emma's earring."

"Excuse me?" Logan asked.

"I was just telling my granddaughter. I used to make lures for my husband."

The General blinked, maintaining his eyelids shut for a fraction longer than usual. For an instant, Logan thought he saw relief in the man's eyes.

"That was right about the time I lost one of my Aunt Emma's earrings. They were my favorite too. It must have gotten snagged on the lure and I didn't notice."

"I remember, dear." The General blinked again. "That was right about the time your finger got infected from a hook jab."

"Yes. Not long after that you switched to live bait."

Now it all made sense to Logan. To spare his wife any further injury indulging his hobby, the man had switched to live bait. Every day he liked the General more than the day before. His grandfather and this man did sneaky well.

CHAPTER FOURTEEN

"You look amazing."

"Thank you." Heaven knows Rose had spent way more time in front of the mirror and discarded more clothing options than she normally would have if Logan Buchanan wasn't attending tonight's final event. Unlike two hours ago, now she was sure that settling on the chiffon gown with the sweetheart neckline, cap sleeves, and yards of swirling fabric had been the right choice.

"Everything looks perfect." Logan casually scanned the crowded hall. "And the silent auction seems very popular."

"I hope so. The wildlife center is a good cause. The new hospital received so many donations from all over New England that it's going to open ahead of schedule, but not as many people get sentimental over saving jealous pelicans."

"Excuse me?"

Rose waved her hand. "Never mind, I'm a little nervous."

"Here." Logan tugged her into his personal space and placed a slow, gentle kiss on her cheek. "For good luck."

She smiled. "I may need a few more of those."

"Any time." He grinned back.

"Rose!" Nadine came rushing across the floor, pivoting around tables, and practically leaping over chairs. "We have a problem."

The four most terrifying words on the night of a big event. "What's wrong?"

"I just heard over the police scan."

"You're listening to the scan now?" Rose squeaked.

Nadine rolled her eyes. "Be glad I did. We've got a heads up."

"Nadine, would you please skip a Chapter and get to the Epilogue."

"There's been an accident about ten minutes south of town. Big pile up. One car with Boston license plates."

Quickly Rose ran an inventory of any family members that would have Boston plates.

"The auctioneer is on his way to the hospital."

Auctioneer. Rose didn't know if she should sigh with relief that her family was well, or crawl into a corner and cry. "Great. Just great."

"I know, honey. What do you want me to do?"

"I don't suppose you have a spare auctioneer on speed dial."

Poor Nadine looked stricken. "I can get Judge Callahan to lend us his gavel. Will that help?"

Her *no* tumbled over Logan's *yes*.

"Are you crazy?" she asked him. "What good is a gavel without an auctioneer?"

"You do it." He actually said that with a straight face.

"You are crazy." She sucked in a deep breath through her nose and out through her mouth. Just the way Violet had taught her. It wasn't helping.

Logan grabbed hold of her hand. "Think about it. Everyone from town loves you and your family, and all the fishermen are mostly here to drink and have a good time."

"None of that is making me feel any better. Except maybe the drink part. I might have to change my policy of imbibing while on the clock."

"I'm serious. You are a formidable woman."

"Listen to him." Nadine waved a thumb in Logan's direction. "The man is smarter than he looks."

Rose nearly spit with laughter at the startled look on Logan's face. She could almost see the cogs in his mind turning as he debated whether to take issue with the pseudo insult or continue on his crazed mission for her to replace the auctioneer. The way he barely shook his head before facing her again told her which argument had won.

"You are good with people, you are not afraid of crowds, you have a sense of humor, and when in command, you can talk pretty fast."

"I beg your pardon."

"Honey." Nadine placed a hand on her forearm. "Like it or not, you're a city girl and all of you can talk fast."

"Not that fast."

"Fast enough," Nadine added.

"I don't know." Was she actually considering this? Could she pull it off? No. It was crazy.

"You can," Logan said.

What? Was the man a mind reader now too?

"I'll be here if you need me."

A lot of good that would do her. She'd probably see him in the audience and all intelligent thought would spill out her ears again. Just look at her now. He was standing too close. Her synapses had to be frying because she was actually considering doing as he said.

"We'll give away a few rounds of drinks," Nadine suggested. "Liquor 'em up good and they'll never know you're not the real thing."

Rose shot her grandparents' friend an are-you-kidding glare.

"Hey, you're the fundraising pro. At least it will loosen their wallets," Nadine defended.

That much was true.

"You can do it." Logan squeezed her hand and nodded. "I know you can."

Damn that man and her rattled brains. Rose sucked in a deep breath, waited for sanity to settle in, and when no brilliant ideas came to mind, she exhaled and nodded her head. "For better or worse, I hope you're right.

• • • •

So did he. First thing on Logan's agenda, he needed to pay for a round of drinks for the house. He had no idea what she meant by jealous pelicans, but all that mattered to him was that this charity mattered to her. He was pretty sure at least Lucy would approve. Wasn't it Dolly Levi who had said money, like manure, should be spread around to help young things grow?

"You look rather serious." The General came to his side and raised a glass to him. "Smile. It's a good night. Win or lose, you did well. Your grandfather would be pleased."

"Thank you." Logan looked over the man's shoulder. Normally he would have loved to exchange stories of his grandfather, but he wanted to get to the bar tab before Nadine. "Do you know who the lead caterer is?"

"Yes." The General spun about. "Barb Miller is in charge." He waved a finger at an older woman in black slacks and a black button-down dress shirt.

"Got it. Give me a minute. And," he paused already in motion, "thanks."

"Sure thing," the General called after him.

Across the hall he could see Nadine surveying the room, no doubt searching for the same person he was. Only he was already closing in on Barb. "Excuse me."

"Yes?" She looked up with a smile. "Do you need something?"

"Actually, I do. I'd like to pick up the tab for a round of drinks."

"You would." Her tone dripped with incredulity.

"I would. And I'd like to remain anonymous. I'd rather no one found out who donated."

"Of course." Barb smiled but he could see her calculating how to make her escape.

"Maybe this will help." Pulling his wallet from his pocket, he retrieved his black limitless credit card.

Like a cartoon character, Barb's eyes took over her face with shock. And even still, it took another fifteen minutes of fast talking before she finally agreed to run the card. Not until the surprisingly large by the glass price had been approved did she fall all over herself promising her eternal silence. He had a feeling if he'd asked for it, she might have thrown in her first born.

A finger tapping on the mic reverberated in the noisy room.

"Is it on?" Rose's voice asked.

Several key people nodded.

"Ladies and Gentlemen, the silent auction will be closing in fifteen minutes. Last chance to take these wonderful donations home with you tonight. Fifteen minutes. Thank you."

He stood in place, admiring the way her gown flowed as she walked across the stage. With every few steps, some person or other stopped her, chatted her up. Her smile never faltered. A time or two he heard her calm, reassuring laugh all the way where he stood. She could charm the skin off a snake and he meant that in a good way. When she reached the top of the steps, she paused to scan the room. His heart rate kicked up a notch as he thought how nice it would be if she were looking for him. Logic dictated she needed the caterer, or the lead volunteer, or a bartender, or maybe the judge and his gavel, but still it didn't hurt to pretend for a little while she wanted him.

"Can you imagine that?" Nadine came up behind him.

Tearing his gaze away from Rose, he turned to Nadine. "Imagine what?"

"Someone, an anonymous donor, paid for a good number of free drinks."

"Did they?" He hoped his surprise sounded sincere. "An animal lover?"

"I suppose." Nadine's plastic smile told him she wasn't convinced, or maybe it was her police background that made her generally suspicious of just about anyone.

"There you are." Rose tapped him on the shoulder.

If he could have done a back flip and not look foolish, he would have. She'd been looking for him. "Right here. You're doing great."

"Announcements and charming money away from people with too much of it is easy. It's the next part that I'm not so sure about."

"Here." Nadine grabbed a champagne glass from the tray of a passing waiter. "This will help."

Rose waived her hands in front of her face. "After the auction."

"If you say so." Nadine shrugged and took a sip from the glass herself. "Good stuff."

"Do you have the gavel?" Rose asked.

"Oops!" Nadine chuckled. "Be right back."

The woman scurried away and Rose shook her head. "That Merry Widows club can be dangerous."

"Merry Widows? Isn't Nadine married to Ned?"

Rose chuckled. "She is, but what's a breathing husband among friends."

"I see." He didn't, but he'd learned a long time ago figuring out how a woman's mind worked, any woman of any age, was not in his skill set. His father had taught him if Mama ain't happy, nobody's happy, and Logan figured that was about as much as he needed to understand about women.

"Here you go." Nadine came hurrying back, waving the gavel in front of her.

"I think I'm going to throw up," Rose muttered as the gavel slapped against her palm.

"You can do this," he encouraged. If only she could see herself through his eyes. Quickly tapping and scrolling through his phone he scanned his options, downloaded, and handed her the phone. "This is a voice recognition app to help auctioneers keep track of the bidding. It should help."

Her hand flew to her chest and he wasn't sure if she was going to laugh or throw up, but she slowly took the phone, shaking her head. "Only you."

"Ladies and gentlemen," Cindy's voice came over the mic, "it's my personal pleasure to thank you all for coming tonight."

While her cousin continued warming up the crowd with stories of the animals and the value of the wild life center, Rose took in several deep breaths and squeezed his hand.

"Don't forget to exhale. It doesn't work if you don't exhale. You'll just pass out."

"And that's a bad thing?" she teased.

He leaned over and kissed her on the check. "For good luck."

"Your auctioneer for the night, Rose Preston!"

Applause filled the room as Rose made her way to the podium. She could do this.

Rose described the first item up for auction. An eighteenth-century bed warmer. A bona fide antique very possibly from one of Paul Revere's contemporaries. The bidding started at one hundred dollars and the room grew horribly quiet. It might have helped if she'd started with something the men wanted, like the antique fishing gear he'd donated, but a bed warmer it was. He raised his bidding card.

The relieved smile that spread across Rose's face was worth every penny that contraption would cost him.

"One ten, do I hear one ten? Ladies and gentlemen, if nothing else I bet it makes great popcorn."

The room burst out in laughter and she managed to finagle two hundred dollars for the eighteenth-century popcorn maker.

The next item went more smoothly but not high enough as far as he was concerned. A new strategy might be necessary. When someone took interest, and a moment of silence fell, he raised his card. Apparently, what he'd heard, that it's the exhilaration of the competition that pushes people to spend too much at auctions, seemed to have merit. The room was filled with competitors and by the time the first edition of *Adventures of Huckleberry Finn* came up, he'd only accidentally bought two items he had no idea what to do with. All for a good cause.

"We'll start the bidding for this timeless treasure at five thousand dollars."

Immediately, Logan raised his card and the sweet smile she'd flashed him at his first bid had slowly slipped into a hint of a scowl as he bid on item after item. He couldn't swear to it, but he was pretty sure the lady was concerned about his bank account.

"I have five thousand, do I have six? Six, do I have seven?"

Several bidders had joined the frenzy. Who knew there were so many literary lovers in the room? When the bidding reached fifteen thousand all but two people bowed out. A balding man sucking on an unlit cigar whose wife elbowed him with every price increase, and himself.

"Sixteen thousand, I have sixteen. Seventeen."

Lightning cracked outside and a thunderous clap rattled the windows. The drive back to Hart Land was going to be interesting.

"Eighteen, do I hear eighteen?"

His card went up and her searing glare could have burned a hole through him.

"I have eighteen. Nineteen. Twenty," she went on. At twenty-one, the balding old man turned to his younger counterpart and threw a scowl that would have withered even the stormiest of generals. Baldie's wife huffed so loud Logan could almost hear it from where he stood.

"Sold for twenty thousand dollars to number one forty-nine."

The gavel pounded and the room erupted in applause then immediately died down with the next item up for bid. When the last item was sold, Rose set the gavel down on the podium, thanked the attendees for their generosity and strode off the stage as if she hadn't a care in the world.

The minute she set foot on the wooden floors, her gaze met his and he could see a storm brewing in her eyes to match the one outside. "Hi. You did great."

"How much have you had to drink?"

"Excuse me?" He held up his hands. One empty, the other with the bidding card that made her cringe.

"I'm sorry." She squeezed her eyes tightly closed, then opened them and forced a smile as she settled her gaze on him again. "You seem perfectly sober and not the least bit worried about all the items you bought."

"Only five."

"Yes. Five. And what exactly do you plan to do with an eighteenth-century bed warmer?"

"Make popcorn, of course."

That made her laugh.

"I said you'd be great. That joke broke the ice."

"Your starting bids didn't hurt."

He hefted his shoulder in an effort at a casual shrug. "Glad I could help."

"Yeah, me too." The corners of her mouth inched up in just a hint of a smile.

Edna the owner of Buy the Book approached. "I am so happy to see someone who appreciates good literature win the first edition."

"I don't know about good literature, but I certainly appreciate Mark Twain. Just seeing the book brought back happy memories."

"Excellent taste." The woman beamed.

"But, I must admit I bought the book for a gift."

"A gift?" The bookstore owner's eyebrows arched high over startled brown eyes. "That's quite a special gift."

"It's for quite a special person." He cast a short glance in Rose's direction. "Who definitely appreciates literature."

Edna's gaze darted from him to Rose and back. A knowing smile bloomed and she nodded, placing her hand on his. "I understand, but I really must run along now. There's quite a bit of hubbub about my other first editions."

When he shifted his gaze from Edna's departing back to Rose, she was staring at him with a different kind of fire in her eyes. "You're giving the book away?"

He nodded. "If you'll accept it."

"Me?" Her eyes popped open wide with surprise.

All he could do was nod. Words seemed to fail him.

She shook her head. "I can't. That's a very—"

"I promise you it will be easier reading than *Anna Karenina.*"

"Anything is easier reading than Tolstoy, but I can't."

"It would make me very happy if that book could bring you even a portion of the pleasure it gave me."

Her head tipped sideways as she carefully studied him. "I don't understand you. Why would you give something so very valuable away to someone you barely know?"

"I know you better than you think." Even as he said them, he realized the words didn't come out quite right. "What I mean is—"

"It's all right. I understand what you meant. I agree it's a lovely gift. I'm still not sure I can accept." She smiled. "But thank you."

Another round of lightning and thunder shook the room, making that sweet smile slip. "Glad this waited till the tournament was over to besiege us."

Logan nodded. "Hopefully it will ease up tomorrow when most folks go home."

Her head whipped around. "You're going home tomorrow?"

"No. Are you?"

"No." She sighed. "I am sticking around for the clean-up and any loose ends that need tying up, and then I want at least one full day with the family."

"I see." That didn't give him much time.

"How long are you staying?" she asked softly.

"I'm not sure."

"I know the General would love to have you stick around a few more days. He's always interested in a good whist partner."

"The General?"

Her gaze drifted behind him a moment before locking on him again. "*I'd* love it if you'd stay a little longer."

His heart was officially doing handstands. "Then I guess I'm staying on."

CHAPTER FIFTEEN

"I'm not much for clichés, but if this downpour continues we're going to have to draw straws for who builds the arc and who collects the animals." Rose stared at the constant rain. The first storm had come and gone the first night of the tournament. Fortunately, it had tapered off as forecasted before the second day of fishing, but by the time the banquet was in full swing, so were the rains again. They hadn't stopped all day yesterday and if this kept up, getting home to Boston tomorrow was going to be a nightmare.

"Nonsense," Grams tsked. "The whole point of the rainbow is the promise never to destroy the earth by flood. We won't need an arc."

Callie kicked her toe against the floor and set the rocker moving. "Last night the news said the rains should be moving north at a pretty fast clip. Tapering off here by later this afternoon."

"I saw that too," Rose said. "They're predicting it's going to get pretty ugly by the time it hits the Canadian border."

"Good thing it's not winter, the Canucks would be up to their chins in snow and ice." Lucy turned, shaking her head, and went back inside.

The General remained still, his face tilted skyward. "I've looked at a lot of nasty skies in my day. I don't see this easing up any time soon. If anything, the rain's getting heavier. If the wind picks up any more we're going to have a problem."

"Oh my." Grams pushed to her feet and slowly moved to her husband's side.

It wasn't often that concern darkened her grandmother's countenance. She had a way of always looking to the brighter side of a situation. How could we enjoy lemonade if we never had any lemons type of thinking. "It does bring back memories."

"Not good ones." The General folded his wife's hand in his. "I'd like to get a good look at that weather map myself."

"I can turn on the local news," Callie mentioned. "Get an updated forecast."

Shaking his head, the General turned to face the folks sitting around the enclosed winter porch. "Not the little Doppler that they show viewers. The big picture."

"I might be able to help." Logan pulled out his phone and swiped a few things. "Though it would be easier if I had access to a computer."

Callie jumped from the rocker. "I have my laptop in my bag by the steps. I'll be back in a second."

"Bring my poncho and boots too," the General called after her.

"Oh Harold," Grams muttered softly, "maybe that won't be necessary. Maybe it's not that bad and the TV people are right and it will all blow over."

Poppy and her mother came scurrying up the walk. The wind practically blew the two women and their umbrellas through the porch door.

"Wind's picking up and the water's rising," Aunt Virginia blurted. "Beach is covered."

"High tide?" Logan asked.

The General nodded. "Yes, but add almost two days and three nights of nonstop rain, the last thirty-six hours coming in solid sheets, and that's why the beach is under water."

Callie set her laptop in front of Logan and in a few seconds his fingers flew on the keyboard. With every click of his mouse, the lines on his forehead deepened. He'd pause to scan the screen, then tap on the keys some more. "Blast."

"What's wrong?" Rose asked.

"I'm blocked. Give me a minute." Logan's gaze never left the screen.

Standing over the Texan's shoulder, the General's eyes widened. "You're hacking into government satellites." It wasn't a question, and Rose was pretty sure she saw more pride than shock in her grandfather's eyes.

Focusing on the screen in front of him, Logan blew out a hard breath and leaned back. "The storm isn't going to move out as forecasted."

The way his back teeth clenched and the muscled cords in his neck tightened, Rose knew whatever he was looking at was not good. "There's more, isn't there?"

He nodded. "It isn't going anywhere. It's stalled dead smack on top of us and according to these images, this little sprinkle isn't the worst of it."

"I didn't think so." The General's shoulder's straightened and his chin lifted. Rose had just witnessed her grandfather leave the room and General Harold Hart USMC enter.

"It's Hurricane Adelaide all over again," Virginia mumbled under her breath.

"Could be." The General shrugged into the rain poncho that his granddaughter held out for him.

"Hurricane?" Poppy tipped her head in confusion. "We're in the mountains."

"But the outlying storms can be just as…serious," Logan stumbled over his last words. Not that Rose needed to be told what he'd really wanted to say. "We should notify the town officials. From what I just saw, this is going to get very ugly."

The General nodded. "I need to get outside and see for myself. We may not have much time. Lucy," the General turned to the woman standing stone-faced in the doorway, "call the mayor. Put Logan on the line so he can tell her what he just told us. Then tell her we'll need access to the district warehouse. And most likely so will anyone else with a house close to the shore."

Without a word, Lucy turned and rushed into the house, following orders.

"If you'll give me one minute I'll go with you. You may want some back up."

The General nodded. "The assist is appreciated."

Logan looked to Rose in silent request for another raincoat as he followed Lucy into the kitchen.

"I'll get him some extra boots. Those cowboy boots may be pretty but they're not worth a plug nickel in this weather." Poppy bolted around her mother.

Grams gently patted her husband's arm. "Should I call the rest of the girls?"

His gaze on the hall Logan had disappeared into, the General shook his head. "At this point it's likely best for them to stay where they are."

Lucy came running back inside. "That man is good. Only took him a minute of very precise words before the Mayor said she would authorize a media alert. Per Logan's suggestion, all citizens will be advised to stay put except for folks on the shore. They're being told to move to higher ground if at all possible. Also, she's putting the word out for all local emergency volunteers to report and help deliver sand bags and be on the ready for rescue operations."

The General nodded and looked to Logan, hurrying toward him, buttoned up to his chin. "Ready?"

"I'm coming too." Rose turned to get another slicker.

"No." Her grandfather shook his head. "I'd rather you check with the guests we have left and ask if they'd be willing to help. Wouldn't hurt to gather up all the rain gear we have in one place for easier access too."

Rose didn't have to ask needed for what. When Hurricane Sandy had torn through the east coast, her mom had told her stories from when she was a little girl at the lake and the aftermath of Hurricane Adelaide. The neighbors had banded together sandbagging the cottages on Hart Land and nearby. Only her grandfather's insistence that they board windows as well had saved his and his friend's property from more damages. But that time they'd had more warning. Now she wasn't so sure if time was on their side.

● ● ● ●

"Damn," the General muttered.

Visibility was seriously limited. Even in the middle of the day, the thick layer of clouds had darkened the afternoon to dusk. From indoors it had appeared the rain was pouring down in sheets, but trudging down the paths to the shoreline was almost like battling a fire hose. No wonder the retired Marine was concerned. There was only so much water land could absorb, and judging by the way his boots sank, Hart Land had passed its limit.

At the water's edge the General muttered another curse. They'd barely passed the last cabin that should have still been a good walk to the sandy retreat and instead the choppy lake rolled over their boots. Silently, the retired general executed a ninety degree turn and marched across the land with the gusto of a much younger Marine. Not till they stopped at the stone wall by the creek did Logan realize the Point was almost completely under water as well. Just how much water had Mother Nature dumped in the last twenty-four hours?

Turning to his left, the General walked the wall to the end. With the water so high, there was no leaning over to untie a boat. "You do that one, I'll do this one."

Logan untied the boat at the end. He could see why the old man would prefer to take his chances in the open water than against a stone wall.

The paddle and fishing boats free from the Point, Logan followed the General as he walked up the wall creek side. He didn't need to see or hear the man to know what he was the thinking. The small creek had swelled to a rushing river. He knew people who would pay big bucks to ride down that sucker. What he liked even less than the increased flow of water was the debris floating along.

Lips pressed in a tight line, the General shook his head. "We'll have to secure this. I've got sandbags in the winter shed."

The two continued to walk a few more feet. He knew the General was checking the integrity of the wall as much as he was keeping tabs on the sporadic cluster of branches coming their way. If the storm was breaking branches from the aged timber the flow of twigs and sticks would be steady, the occasional limb—leaves and all—would be floating past him. These twigs and sticks were bare and clustered and the flow spread too far apart. It took a few more minutes before the pattern began to make sense to Logan, and he didn't like it one bit. "How many bags do you have? Because if I'm guessing right, we're going to need a lot."

Brows buckled, the General cast his gaze upstream and then back. "I think we have enough."

A clap of thunder and flash of lightning had Logan looking off in the distance. He'd seen some pretty dark clouds over the Texas horizon, but he'd never expected to see anything as black as a gulf storm. "We need to move fast. When those clouds roll all the way in they are going to drop Niagara Falls on us."

The General followed his gaze.

"When it does," Logan continued, "the dam is going to give way. We may not have much time."

"Dam?" The General turned his attention back up stream and even in the shadow of the storm Logan could see the change in the old man's eyes the minute he realized what Logan had. "Shit. I take that back. I don't have enough sand bags stored up for that. We need to get moving faster than I thought." The old man took off at a trot. "Pull the tether out of the ground. We'll need to collect up anything that can become a projectile."

Logan nodded, yanked the thing out of the soggy dirt as he scrambled by and followed the General up the porch steps. Aided by the wind, the door slammed open. A pile of yellow slickers, boots and rain hats were stacked to one side. Lucy had changed from her usual housedress into jeans. More startling was Mrs. Hart. The woman who usually looked like fashion model from an era long gone wore her sleek silver hair tied back in a short ponytail, jeans and an oversized sweatshirt that announced *Stay Safe, Sleep with a Marine.* If the situation hadn't been so dire he would have laughed.

"Shed's unlocked," Mrs. Hart told her husband. "Cole called. His chief gave him permission to come help us bag. Ralph and the guest from the Elm have already taken a load. They're starting with the first cabin. Sealing the door."

The General looked to Lucy. "You and Rose pull up the volleyball net." He turned to Poppy and his daughter. "You two start moving all the chairs to the shed."

Shaking off the rain, Callie came through the door. "I'm here."

"Good. You can bring in the bocce balls."

The five women nodded and took a step back ready to do as tasked.

"We're going to need more bags." He turned to his wife. "Call Jake. See if he has any sand bags at the store, though I doubt it, or sacks he can stand to lose. Then call Cole and see if he can pick up Alan and Eric on his way. We could use the extra manpower. There may not be much time."

"Time for what?" his wife asked tentatively.

The General scooped her hand in his. "It looks like a beaver dam up creek is coming apart from all the rain. It's bound to break apart when the next phase of the storm hits. If we're right and it's the dam that's been halfway up the mountain for years, the thing is massive. All the water—"

"Will come over the wall, straight for us," Fiona Hart stated matter-of-factly.

Rose's gaze darted from her grandparents to his. The woman he'd grown incredibly fond of—okay, had come to care for, okay, who was he kidding—the woman he was falling head over boot heels for stood as proud and calm as her remarkable grandmother. She studied his face a moment and then gave an almost imperceptible nod. "We'd better get cracking."

And just like that she was off to save the day. Didn't matter if she was dealing with an art show, an auction, or a natural disaster. With or without her precious binders, the woman knew how to get the job done. There was nothing about Rose Preston that didn't amaze him. Silently kicking himself out of his thoughts and into action, he turned to the General. "Let's start raising up that wall."

The General nodded and once again marched forward, through the house and out the back door. They had a high stakes mission to accomplish and they'd better not fail. The dam was giving way, and when it finally blew, the whitewater rapids of Colorado were going to look like a trickle compared to creek threatening to flood Hart Land.

CHAPTER SIXTEEN

By the time reinforcements arrived, the women had successfully battled the wind and rain and quickly cleared the grounds of anything that could fly into a window, or land in the lake, or worse, propelled by wind power, kill someone. Virginia Nelson had reached out to every guest to move them to cabins on higher ground. The family's friend and neighbor Ralph, along with some of the guests, had used most of the stored sand bags to stop the rising water from seeping into the cabins under the doors. So far, the lake's edge was licking closer to the buildings than anyone liked.

With help from the cousins' husbands and fiancés, one row of the remaining sand bags had been stacked along the stone wall as far as the main road. With the creek already less than a foot below the existing wall, if the rain didn't stop soon, Logan wasn't holding out much hope that a single layer would make any difference.

"How many more bags do we have?" Logan leaned into the back of Jake's truck.

From the bed of his pick-up, Jake shoved large sacs toward the tailgate. "We're out of sand. This is feed. Should do the trick."

"It will have to."

The walkie-talkie clipped to Jake's belt chirped. "Jake here."

"It's the beaver dam all right," Cindy announced. While Eric and Cole worked alongside the family, Cindy and Alan had gone to determine how much of a threat the dam was. "The top of the top dam has been compromised. The cascade seems steady though. The roads are mud pits and we can't get any closer. I have no idea if the structure will survive."

He'd been surprised they'd made an attempt at all, but apparently a 'little rain' never hurt anyone.

"All right," Jake sighed. "Be careful coming back."

"We're going to stay at Alan's. From his back room we can keep an eye on the dam. It's not the same as being on top of it, but we'll report any notable change."

"Sounds like a plan. We've got enough people here. Stay dry." Jake hooked the walkie-talkie on his belt again and shook his head. "What a mess."

That about summed it up.

As the pitch of night fully descended, Lucy and Mrs. Hart set up spotlights near the house. They weren't ideal, but the last thing they needed was for someone to go over the side because they couldn't see in front of their faces.

Poppy and Rose lugged the last two feed bags from the truck and hurried past Logan to the wall. It amazed him that in the rushing back and forth, tracking through the soggy grounds, barely able to see two feet in front of them, no one had taken a nose dive in the mud.

"It's not enough." The General had split his time between ensuring his wife and housekeeper remained busy with tasks that would keep them out of the rain, and checking on the progress of the make shift retaining wall. Logan was pretty sure the man was itching to do the heavy lifting himself, but he was smart enough to accept that at his age there were limitations on what a retired Marine could do.

After spending the last couple of hours hauling heavy bags about, no one seemed to care about the constant downpour. Having laid the last bag of feed, the six of them and the handful of guests gathered around the bed of Jake's truck. Before anyone could mention a new plan, high and bright headlights turned onto Hart Land. For the first time in hours one of them cracked a smile.

"Looks like the cavalry is here." Grinning, Cole waved his finger in a half-hearted effort to point at the incoming truck.

"Man, do I know how a duck must feel." Payton, Cole's buddy from the fire department, climbed down and shouted over the wind. "Where do you want these?"

"On the wall would be good but since that truck will sink like an antelope in quicksand, right here will have to do." The General gestured to the side of the paved drive.

"*Here* it is." Payton lifted one arm halfway to his face and then quickly let it fall to the side. Logan knew how the guy felt; more than once he'd had to fight the urge to salute the old guy.

With the help of the volunteers, the bags were neatly stacked to one side and the construction line had begun again before they'd driven off Hart Land. A bitter chill shot down Logan's spine. In Texas, that feeling would have had him checking the tall grass for rattlers. Here, he prayed his fears were far worse than reality.

"Let's get this last load out and then get inside and get dry like the sane people in the world." Jake grabbed a bag in each hand and as if willed by Logan's thoughts, his foot slipped one way and his other foot followed a different direction, landing him flat on his keister.

"That does it. No more stomping about." The General marched to the shed at the back of the house and emerged moments later storming in their direction, carrying several bundles of corded rope. "We're doing this bucket brigade style. And I want the men closest to the water tied together in pairs." Muttering, he added, "Should have done this from the start."

Despite the logic of the safety precaution, Logan had never liked the idea of being tethered to anyone on dry—or sort of dry—land for any reason. Especially not in the dark of night in the middle of the worst storm the lake had seen in almost forty years.

"He's right." Rose moved closer for him to hear. "It's safer at this point."

Had the woman read his mind? Did she know him so well that even under these circumstances she could read his face? Why was it that even standing in the pouring rain under the pressure of a ticking clock, he wanted to lean in and kiss the worried look from her face.

"No." She shook her head and took a step back, just far enough to be out of reach.

Okay, maybe the woman *could* read minds. Or maybe she just wanted to set up the brigade and he was being paranoid. There was no time to debate the idiosyncrasies of losing his mind over a woman. The wall wasn't nearly high enough yet if things got worse before they got better.

A loud crack sounded and all heads snapped toward the mountain top. Louder than the way thunder had been clapping all night, more like the snap of a ginormous match stick, the eerie sound made the hairs on the back of his neck bristle. Match stick. "The dam," he moaned.

Another crack filled the air, Jake's walkie-talkie crackled and Cindy's voice echoed through the static. "The center structure just broke loose. The rest could go any minute. Everyone get the hell inside. Now!"

• • • •

Stunned by the sudden loud pitched crack breaking through the night, everyone stared frozen at the mountain top. Even in the dark of night and pouring rain, the increased sound of rushing water reached Rose's ears. They'd run out of time. Suddenly, four or five men rushed to drop the sandbags they already held at the highest point of the sanded wall and to her horror, instead of heading indoors, all of them grabbed more bags. "We've got to get inside!" She might as well have been talking to the stone wall itself.

Jake paused in front of her. "Go inside."

"No. Not without all of you."

Stopping at her side, Logan parroted Jake's word. "We've got this. You and your cousins go inside. Please."

On the road ahead, headlights bounced against the sheets of rain momentarily catching her and Logan's attention.

"That's not another delivery truck," Logan said. "Who is crazy enough to drive on a night like this."

Rose squinted as if there were any chance in hell she could make out a car model. Another boom sounded, breaking the hum of steady pouring rain, followed by a roar. A very loud roar. Without any effort, suddenly there was no need to strain to see. The foamy white of the cascading water appeared across the road and up the hill, rushing down like an oil slick kid on a water park slide. Except this was no amusement park, more like a dangerous rapid river.

"Oh my God." Logan dropped the bags he held. "The driver doesn't see it."

Voices, barely audible over the rushing water, shouted as every able-bodied person forgot about the bags and ran to the main road, repeatedly screaming, "Stop!"

The car, that Rose could now see was an antique sports car of some kind, continued to roll along, approaching the roaring creek.

"That's Marylou Parker's Pontiac Firebird," her grandfather shouted over the roar, rushing up the hill beside her. "She's deaf as a tree stump and terrified to drive in the rain. What in blue blazes is she doing out on this of all nights?"

The rushing waters seemed to pick up speed as the torrent reached the main road. Rose's heart nearly stopped. The world seemed to turn in slow motion. Everyone froze in place. Eyes rounded with horror as the old Pontiac reached the overpass at the same time as the deluge of rushing water passed under and over the road.

"Oh God," Rose repeated. More of a prayer than a cry.

The movie reel still rolling in slow motion, the rushing waters slid under the vehicle like surreal tendrils, lifting the car off the road and ever so slowly nudging it over the side. Carrying it away in the rush like the hero football player by a crowd of adoring fans after winning a championship game. Except there would be no winners here.

Steps ahead of her, half the men were already running alongside the makeshift wall, the shouts now pleading for Marylou to open a window.

Water sloshed over the sides of the sandbagged wall in some places and gushing in others spewed gallons of water and debris across Hart Land. A log almost as big as her caught Poppy's legs from behind and knocked her off her feet, unforgiving waves of water flowing over her limp body.

The General may be old, but the man still had the instincts of a Marine. Or maybe those of a loving grandfather. The closest one to her, he had Poppy on her feet and leaning on him with surprising speed and agility. Grams must have seen most of it as she and Lucy came running from the house to bring her inside. Barking, Lady and Sarge trounced in the muddy waters alongside them.

"Point the lights toward the water," her grandfather shouted at her as he turned and hurried toward the running crowd.

It only took a second to realize he meant the mouth of the Point where the rushing waters would dump Marylou and her car. Holding on to the idea that her cousin would be fine in the hands of her grandmother, Rose rushed as fast as the slick muddied grass would allow and turned the spotlights from the creek to the lake.

The glimmer of light reflected off a metal strip of the floating car that had what felt like an insurmountable lead on all the shouting people running after it. Marylou was going to need a miracle.

Cole and Logan reached the Point first. Somehow one of them had gotten hold of a bundle of rope her grandfather had brought out. Standing ankle high in water at the edge of the Point, Logan tied one end of the rope on the metal ladder as Cole tied the other end around his waist.

Thank heaven Cole was here. A fireman by profession, he was the best one to rescue the old woman. The only thing better might have been a professional life guard; after all, how often did firemen have to rescue people under water.

"How long have we got?" Logan asked, just as Rose reached them.

Having secured the knot, Cole kicked off his boots and looked up. "Five minutes. If we're lucky, maybe a couple more."

Lifting her gaze to the lake, Rose could see that at the mouth of the creek, the force of the rushing waters had pushed the car to the side and it had stopped about twenty feet from the edge of the Point. Ten minutes didn't seem like much time.

"Is she climbing out?" a voice asked from over Rose's shoulder.

"Doesn't look that way," Cole answered, then quickly dove into the lake. The water splashed behind him as his feet propelled him slowly forward against the rising water.

"I'll take that end." Logan reached for the rope Jake held beside him.

Staring after Cole and praying for both him and Marylou, it took a few seconds for her to realize that this time Logan was tying the rope around himself not the ladder. He was going in after Cole. The man was a Texan. And a geek. Her heart lurched and lodged in her throat. She wanted to scream *NO* but nothing came out.

• • • •

"This might help." Jake pulled a small tool from his key chain. "Supposed to shatter glass in an emergency. No idea if it works, but..."

Logan nodded, double checked the knotted rope around his waist and looking up, his gaze momentarily locked with Rose. There was no time for comfort; a reassuring smile as he turned and dove in was all he could offer. He wasn't even sure that she could see it in this storm.

The choppy water splashed at his face, robbing him his breath as his head broke through the water. The downpour made visibility in the water even worse than above ground. Thank heaven for the spotlight. Shaking away the excess water, even though in the heavy storm and at this distance the light was pretty dim, at least he was able to spot the car and Cole. Already the front end was pointed downward and the hood was completely under water. He pushed forward, losing sight of Cole as the fireman disappeared under the water, finally springing up on the other side. The doors had to be locked. Cole was using both his feet to kick in the passenger side window, but wasn't getting enough leverage.

As Logan reached the car, Cole reappeared on this side. The driver, an older woman as expected, was awake but not moving.

"She's probably in shock," Cole shouted. "I'm going to try the rear window."

"Jake gave me this."

Cole's eyes lit up at the handheld tool. Apparently the thing might just work and from Cole's expression, he knew what to do with it. Within moments the glass was shattered. Cole had already removed his t-shirt and wrapped it around his hand to clear away all the shards of glass.

Following his lead, Logan stripped off his shirt and laid it across the edge for added protection when the woman climbed out.

"Marylou!" Cole shouted, but the woman barely reacted. "We have to get you out. Can you unbuckle your seat belt? I need you to give me your arms."

Nothing. It looked like the only way to get Marylou out alive was going to be giving her a shove. "I'll try the back window."

Already leaning into the car and cutting off her straps with that same tool, Cole continued shouting at the woman and Logan said a silent prayer. He'd done a lot of MacGyver moves on the ranch through the years, but none ever involved life and death.

Around the rear he lifted himself onto the bumper and shifted around until his arms held all his weight. One kick. Two. Three and the glass cracked. Yes! Another kick and both his feet were inside. Another minute and so was he, and a barking dog, and lord help him. A little boy! *Please let him be sleeping and not injured.*

Cole's head whipped around at the dog's barks. Apparently he hadn't noticed the back seat either. Logan checked the boy's pulse. Strong. Thank heaven. The dog barked again. The boy didn't budge, but at least the bark seemed to snap Marylou into reality.

"Rocky!" she shouted.

"Come on, Marylou. Reach for me," Cole encouraged.

"What happened?"

"You got swept into the lake. Reach for me."

"Oh my God, Jimmy."

"We know, Marylou, but I can't get anyone else out until I get you out. Reach for me."

Marylou had twisted but struggled to crawl through. Logan squirmed between the dog and boy, both harnessed into the backseat, and positioned himself on the passenger side. "Sorry about this, ma'am." Placing his hands low on her derriere, he gave the woman a gentle but firm nudge.

"Oh!" Marylou shrieked as Cole pulled her the rest of the way out.

"You got this?" Cole asked.

"Go." Though he had no idea how he was going to swim in this storm with a little boy and his dog. "I sure hope you can dog paddle."

CHAPTER SEVENTEEN

ow long had it been since Logan disappeared into the car? Rose's heart slammed against her rib cage with more force than she'd ever felt before.

"Breathe." Lily squeezed her arm and spoke softly at her ear.

So consumed by concern for Logan, Rose had almost forgotten that Lily's husband was risking his life to save a stranger as well.

"They'll be okay." Lily's grip tightened. If that was for Rose's benefit or her own she didn't know but she was damn happy to have her cousins at her side.

"She's out!" Iris shrieked from Rose's other side.

"And she's moving around!" Lily released her hold on Rose and did a fist pump.

Eric and Jake stood on either side of the ladder and began pulling the rope in to help bring Cole and Marylou to shore, but where was Logan?

Why wasn't he coming out?

Cole and Marylou were almost to the Point. Rose kicked off her boots and standing in bare feet just inside the stone walled edge, kept her gaze on the car. Still no sign. Why did Cole leave him?

"What are you thinking?" Lily grabbed her arm again.

"Something's wrong."

"Cole will go back. He's almost here. Or one of the others. They're stronger swimmers."

"I'm a good swimmer," she insisted.

"We all are. But they're stronger."

Her mouth hung open ready to give one last protest when a cheer erupted from the ladder. At first she thought it was the safe rescue of Marylou, but Cole had yet to reach the ladder. Swinging around to face the water again she saw why everyone had cheered. Apparently she wasn't the only one worried about what was taking so long. Logan emerged, not from the side window like Cole, but from the rear window, and not alone.

The three men strained to get Marylou to the top of the ladder and into Fiona Hart's waiting arms. She and Callie were in charge of triage. Hopefully Marylou and Poppy would be the only two casualties of the night. And hopefully neither was serious.

In the few seconds Rose had shifted her gaze to Cole and Marylou, Logan had gone from the car into the water and was now being pulled to shore the way they'd done with the earlier rescue. All she could see was Logan's face and a bundle on his back.

With Cole on this end of the rope now, as well as Eric and Jake, they pulled Logan in faster than with only two men, but not fast enough for Rose's liking. Why didn't they pull hard…er. She blinked, twice, as Logan came more clearly into view. He didn't just have a bundle on his back. A little boy clung to his neck, but not with fear; the kid was laughing like the proverbial hyena.

"Look at that!" Lily pointed. "Oh my lord. He's got a dog too!"

Sure enough, paddling alongside him, she could see a canine muzzle poking out above the water. "What the hell?"

Once Logan and company reached the stone wall, Jake held onto the rope, Eric reached down to retrieve the four-legged victim, and Cole loosened the rope to pull the child from Logan's back. Keeping a hold on the youngster's hand, Cole set him on his feet inside the edge of the wall.

Logan propelled himself off the ladder and over the wall, coming to stand by the boy.

"Can we do that again?" the kid asked gleefully.

Tension rolled from everyone's shoulders as the group of stressed adults let out a choral laugh from deep down in their belly.

Standing ankle high in water, Logan kneeled in front of the boy and tussling his wet hair, smiled down. "Maybe on a sunny day. Without the car."

• • • •

"No one is going anywhere." Fiona Hart looked pointedly at each of her grandchildren. Not a single one dared contradict the beloved family matriarch.

"At least it's a big house with lots of rooms." Eric slipped his arm around his wife. This was only the second time Logan had met Iris. The first was briefly at the auction. When he'd heard her described as a native New Yorker he had to admit that the Texan in him expected the uppity worst from her. To his surprise, she was as nice as all the cousins. Every one of them had rolled up their sleeves and pitched in. Even Poppy with her bruised legs had insisted on helping tend to Mrs. Parker and her grandson until the paramedics could get through. Fortunately, in the chaos of the rescue, Lady and Sarge stepped in to do their share, keeping the dog Rocky in line.

And despite the pounding rain, when the dam broke threatening Hart Land, Cindy and Alan descended the mountain to render aid where needed. After the unexpected water rescue, the threat of flooding didn't seem to hold as much power over anyone at Hart House. The main house was high enough to avoid risk, and there wasn't a basement in New England that didn't have its issues with water now and again.

Instead of continuing to work on raising the wall in the pouring rain once the rush of the dam break had passed, the members of the family had been dispersed to different rooms in the charming Victorian, showered, changed into dry clothes, and two by two reappeared in the heart of the home. The kitchen.

Earlier in the storm, when Cole arrived, having picked up Eric on his way, Iris and the kids had stopped for Cindy, and Alan had already been on his way down the mountain when Cole put out the call for help. The concept of circling the wagons was still strong in this clan. Regardless of Fiona Hart's decree that the family was to remain close to the nest, Logan had the feeling no one had had any other plan in mind.

"I know it's well past supper time," Lucy stood center of the massive island, a bit like King Arthur holding court at the round table, "but is anyone hungry?"

Arms shot up.

"That's what I thought." The woman who was clearly more than a housekeeper slapped her hands together and rubbed enthusiastically. "One pot luck midnight buffet coming up."

The sound of sliding chairs shifting filled the room. Lily and Cindy headed for the back freezer, Iris and Poppy reached for aprons, even the men moved about the house not like in laws but like family by blood. Plates were removed from cupboards, silverware from drawers, and Logan looked to Rose carrying a basket of condiments to the other room.

Pushing to his feet, he met her at the dining room door. "Anything I can do to help?"

She shook her head. "You and Cole are relieved of duty for this one."

He hadn't noticed that of all the men, Cole was the only one absent.

"Is he all right?"

Rose's smile took over her face. "While everyone else hit the showers, he got waylaid corralling one of the strays and her litter. Apparently firemen rescue cats from more than just trees. He should be down any minute."

"I'd like to help." He took a step closer.

Her gaze softened and his heart swelled. Inside the old car there had been a moment when he struggled with the latch on the little boy's car seat and the Firebird had slid deeper and the water rose higher. For a split second it pained him more than he thought, not that he might never see the light of day, but that he might never see those beautiful green eyes again. Hear her voice. Or see that massive binder she used to stay organized. He realized that those sappy chick flicks were true. When you find *the* one, sometimes, you just knew.

"Please?" he added.

A smile teased at the corner of her lips. "Fine. You can help set the table, but if Lucy comes after me you'll have to fend her off."

"Yes, ma'am." He smiled.

Somehow, despite the house filled to the brim with people, he and Rose wound up the only two people in the dining room. He started disbursing the stack of plates someone had left on the table.

"I feel sort of sorry for Mrs. Parker." Rose set the napkins by each plate Logan laid out. "She really loved that car."

He'd been a little surprised to see how upset she'd become when the shock and adrenaline wore off and she'd realized she'd lost the Rockford-mobile, as she called it. He thought only men developed extreme attachments to cars. Though in Mrs. Parker's case it might have been more the attachment to the Rockford Files star James Garner than the actual car. "And James Garner."

Rose chuckled. "I wonder how her grandson will feel when he grows up and realizes he's named after his grandmother's favorite name from a TV show?"

"He probably won't care."

"Yeah, you're probably right."

Done with the dishes, he grabbed a stack of knives and rotated the other way around the table, bumping into Rose as she did the same with the forks. The contact made him stop. Now was his chance. How often were the two of them alone in this family? "What would you think if I were to come to Boston for a visit?"

"You want to come to Boston?" Her eyes widened with surprise. What he didn't know was if it was in a good or bad way.

He nodded. "I've heard so much about your museum. And there's so much history…"

"There is that." She made no effort to move, but the twinkle in her eyes dimmed.

What the hell, in for a penny in for a pound. If she didn't feel the same he might as well find out now. "And you."

"Me?" The sparkle in her eyes returned.

He nodded. "I have a tremendous amount of liberty with my job."

"Telecommute?"

"That, but mostly because I don't need it so my bosses bend over backwards so that I'll stay."

"Would that explain the auction? Or was that about the ranch you own?"

"My family owns. Not me."

"Okay." She set another fork on the table, but stood rooted in place. "I'm afraid I'm a little confused. What exactly are you saying?"

Sucking in a deep breath, he blinked hard and reached for her hands, folding them and the few remaining forks in his. They were so small and soft. "I want to spend more time with you. A lot more time. And if it means spending that time in Boston, my job, my life will let me do that." Her smile widened, giving him courage to take the plunge. "I love you and would like for us to have some more time to discover if you could ever feel the same way."

Her mouth dropped open and then snapped shut. "Love," she whispered.

"I know it's soon. Too soon. And you probably think I'm crazy, but I've been around the block a time or two and I'm smart enough to know you are not only special, you are one of a kind, and—"

She silenced him with her fingertip. Eyes sparkling, she inched closer to him. "I think you're pretty special too. I'd love it if you could spend time in Boston." She grinned up at him. Dropping the forks on the table with a clang, Rose stretched her hands around his neck, brushed her mouth against his and whispered, "Emphasis on love."

If it was humanly possible for his heart to leap for joy, it would. His lips pressed against hers and Logan couldn't think of a single reason to ever return to Texas.

"Oh," a voice exclaimed, followed by the low thud of colliding bodies.

"Ouch. Why are you stopping?" Poppy asked.

Rose pulled away, her cheeks blushing the same shade of pink as her cousin Callie.

"I, uh," Callie looked from Rose to Logan and practically tossed a basket of rolls onto the table. "I'll leave these here." Spinning about, she shoved Poppy forward. "I think I hear Lucy calling."

"But…" Poppy sputtered as her cousin ushered her out the door.

"Sorry about that," Rose said.

"Don't be. Now where were we?"

She raised up on her tippy toes and pressed a gentle kiss on his lips. "Setting the table."

"Right." Somehow nothing seemed more exciting than setting the table with Rose. There wasn't a doubt in his mind, she might have reeled him in, but he'd won the prize. Life was about to get very, very good.

CHAPTER EIGHTEEN ~ EPILOGUE

Peace was clearly over rated. When the entire Hart clan came together, the low hum of friendly banter occasionally bookended by the animated debates of a friendly card game was music to Callie's ears.

"They're here," Poppy yelled into the house. Lucy had been waiting for the last of the cousins in order to put warm the rolls.

The late summer shower had Rose and Logan running hand in hand from the car and pretty much sprinting up the steps.

"Whew." Rose shook off the water and twirled her long hair into a knot at the back of her head. "So much for sunshine and blue skies this weekend."

Hellos and hugs made the rounds. A few shouts from the kitchen, an interrupted card game, and lastly a long, warm greeting from Grams.

"That's tomorrow," Callie offered, fanning out her cards again. "Forecasters predicted sunshine today and scattered showers tomorrow."

"Which means," Poppy smiled, "rain today and sun tomorrow. Got it."

Callie noticed how Logan pulled out Rose's chair and then moved the rocker beside her close enough for them to easily hold hands. Another really nice guy. And if the way he looked at her cousin was any indication, he was a keeper. "How are you liking life in Boston?"

"Different from Texas, but in some ways the same. Everyone talks their own kind of funny."

Rose rolled her eyes and squeezed his hand. "Remind me to tell you the story of my friend Marjorie and Logan's niece Krissy when his brother and family came to visit. Needless to say, a Bostonian pronouncing party like *pohtty* can be seriously confusing to a five year old."

"Oh no." Callie had to laugh at that one. As a high school teacher, she knew from experience that kids of any age put an interesting spin on life.

"Yep." Logan nodded. "She's a smart kid, but a Boston accent was above her skill set."

Cindy looked up from the card game. "I'm curious. What else is different yet similar?

"Within your neighborhood, folks are pretty friendly."

"No they're not." Rose smiled at him. She was another one with that moon pie look on her face. "They're just being nice 'cause they like your accent."

"Oh, and those baby blues have nothing to do with it?" Poppy teased from the card table.

"I beg your pardon. That's my fiancé you're talking about."

"What?" Poppy shrieked in chorus with the cousins on the porch.

Rose squeezed her eyes shut. "Oops."

Like an orchestrated dance routine, chairs pushed back and a deluge of surprised relatives descended on her demanding to see the ring and hear the whole story. Except for Grams. Callie noticed, surrounded by all the fuss, her grandmother rocked in her favorite chair, sipped from a warm cup of tea, and smiled at the youngest Boston granddaughter. Not missing a beat, she turned to the General. Where was the bluster and outrage at the slip of the tongue? "You knew?"

Their grandfather nodded his head, but it was Logan who nudged aside by all the squealing cousins, answered her question. "I may have asked permission."

"May have?"

Logan smiled. It was a nice smile. Not for her, but she could see why Rose found it irresistible. According to her cousin, once he smiled all her brain cells would fry.

"I followed the chain of command."

"Chain of command?" Callie spun about to face the General.

"That would be me and your grandmother," her grandfather said, "followed by Rose's parents."

"Suck up," she whispered in his ear and was pleased when he burst out laughing. Good sense of humor too. He would fit in well with this family. And he didn't waste any time going after what he wanted. In this case, Callie was more than pleased the man wanted Rose. She deserved a good guy. They all did.

"Oh." Cole slapped his future in-law on the back. "Forgot to mention. Mrs. Parker called earlier. She's coming over. Wants to give us a proper thank you."

Logan's brows shot high on his forehead and his gaze immediately darted over to Rose. She shrugged, he twisted his mouth, she raised her brows and Callie shook her head. The two had been together for only a few months and already they communicated entire thoughts without words. What were the odds of that happening twice in one family? Whatever the math, she knew better. She didn't stand a chance.

A golden flash caught the corner of Callie's eye. "Good heavens. She had it restored."

Sure enough, a pristine 1978 Pontiac Firebird with the cat eyes headlights pulled in front of Hart House.

"She did say it was her baby," Logan offered.

Poppy tipped her head, watching the older woman push her seat forward to let someone out of the back seat. "That car is older than we are."

"It's older than most people," Cole chimed in. The General cleared his throat and Cole hurriedly added, "But she loves it."

Two boys slid out from inside Marylou Parker's prize possession. Callie recognized the older boy as one of her students and the younger one as the passenger the night of the crash.

"Hello, Mrs. Parker."

"Please," she told Logan, "call me Marylou. After all, you two saved my life, we're pretty much past formalities."

"Yes, ma'am," Logan and Cole chorused.

She waggled her brows at them and the two men catching on quickly, repeated in unison, "Marylou."

"That's better. I brought these little tokens for you." She whipped out two old fashioned plastic pie trays with handles. Like the car, she'd probably had them longer than most people in the room had been alive. "I know Lucy is one of the best cooks in town, and your Lily can bake circles around any of us in town, but my old-fashioned butter crust apple pie still takes the prize every year at the county fair."

Callie could see from the two men's blank expressions and polite thank you that they had no idea what they'd just been given. The old lady was right. Her sister Lily could bake circles around anyone, but Mrs. Parker's secret apple pie recipe was something even Lily might kill for.

From the satisfied smile on the old woman's face, she knew the men would find out soon enough.

"We were just getting ready for Saturday lunch." Grams smiled. "Why don't you and the boys join us?"

"Oh, no." She shook her head. "I have a few more errands to run and Timmy here is my chaperone. Can you imagine that my children think I might drive off the road again in broad daylight from a little drizzle."

Imagine that, Callie thought to herself. Though in all fairness to the old lady, how often did beaver dams break loose during a storm of the decade?

"Timmy," Marylou snapped. "Would you put that thing away. It's not polite."

"But it's Bait and Fish and I'm almost at level six."

"You play Bait and Fish?" Cole leaned over the boy's shoulder and for the first time since crossing the threshold, the kid finally showed some interest.

"Sure. All my friends do. It's great."

"Glad you like it." Logan smiled at the kid with a little too much enthusiasm for a casual comment.

"All right now," Marylou started, "tell Mr. Buchanan and Mr. McIntyre thank you and we'll be on our way."

To his credit, the teen slid his phone into his pocket and shook Logan's hand first. "Thank you, Mr. Buchanan. Mr. McIntyre. We really are glad you saved my grandma and brother. Even if he is a pain more often than not."

The younger sibling scowled over his shoulder at his brother and then twisted forward again.

"Please call me Logan," Rose's new fiancé told the boy.

The kid's ears almost perked up like a pincher on point. "Logan… McIntyre?"

Logan shook his head and from the broad grin on his face, he seemed to have an idea why the kid looked like a dog who had found his scent. "Buchanan."

"*The* Logan Buchanan?" The kid's voice almost cracked with excitement.

"I don't know about *the*, but I'm Logan Buchanan."

"The guy who designed Bait and Fish?"

Logan nodded and this time it was all the men in the room whose heads snapped in his direction.

"You designed Bait and Fish?" Cole confirmed.

Logan nodded again.

"Holy Christmas." Cole turned to Rose. "Do you realize who you're marrying?"

Rose smiled up at her cousin's husband. "Nicest guy in the world."

Eyes wide and hands waving in Logan's direction, Cole carried on, "Who designed the most popular tech game on the planet right now."

And now the rest of the puzzle from the tournament came together. If he'd designed the most popular game on the planet as Cole claimed, the guy could afford whatever auction items he wanted and move to any city he wanted. So now Callie knew. Rose had found her a good guy, who loved her and was smart too.

Yep, the rest of the single women of the world probably didn't stand a chance. All the good, and nice, and smart ones had to be gone.

From Lily's Recipe Box

ALMOND CRESCENT COOKIES
(German Apple Cake)

What you'll need:

2 cups flour
1 cup unsalted butter (two sticks)
1 cup ground almonds
1/3 cup of sugar
1 teaspoon vanilla

Instructions:

Combine all ingredients and work into a smooth dough so it's not sticky. (if it's too sticky or crumbly a little sour cream might help)
Cool for half an hour in the refrigerator
Take small amount of dough – about a small ice cream scoop size - and form into roll then fold in a half moon/ u shape on a greased cookie sheet (may use parchment paper).
Bake at 350 degrees for 12-15 minutes until slightly brown. (keep an eye on them)
Dust with confectioner's sugar.

Lily's Note: If you're a chocolate fan these cookies taste delish dipped in chocolate!

Excerpt from CALYTRIX

Some days Callie Nelson absolutely loved her work. Other days… not so much. Exchanging her head coach at the high school hat for that of a volunteer coach, being outdoors on a warm summer day, and watching her star player in action made today a good day. If the softball season for the town's summer select league was any sign, and she was the type to place bets, she'd wager the farm on her high school varsity softball team making it all the way to state finals next spring. And Deidra was the key to getting them there. All her players were stars in Callie's eyes, but a few stood out, and Deidra was one of those. For the small mountain high school, this would be the year that having so many seniors was going to pay off. The team would take a hit the following year after so many of them graduated, but for now, the players were the embodiment of a well-oiled machine.

"You're looking awfully pleased with yourself." Callie's sister Cindy, the elder of the Nelson clan, and veterinarian extraordinaire, came up from behind.

Callie dragged her gaze away from the practice field as Deidra came up to bat and smiled at her sibling. "Well, this is a surprise."

"Mrs. Brogan's pet rabbit is under the weather. She says the kids in her summer school class are paying more attention to the sick rabbit than her lessons."

"No surprise there." Callie laughed. Not only had Mrs. Brogan taught her and her sisters when they were in high school, she was pretty sure that the older woman had taught Callie's mom Virginia as well. Heck, she wouldn't be surprised if the old bat had taught the General and her grandmother. Even back when she was a student, Callie had wanted to give the woman new batteries to speed up her lessons. Mrs. Brogan gave a whole new meaning to monotonous monologue. "If I were still in her class, I'd be paying more attention to the rabbit too." Callie slipped her fingers in front of her mouth and smiling, glanced at who might be within earshot. "But you didn't hear me say that."

"Hear you say what?" Cindy swatted her sister lightly across the shoulder as if she were still the naïve sibling in need of big sister correction and chuckled. "But quit picking on that nice old lady."

Shaking her head, Callie glanced over to the game and back. "I won't, but there isn't a soul who has sat through American history that doesn't know Mrs. Brogan could lull a whirling dervish to sleep with her stories of LBJ."

"She did like that man." Cindy sighed, no doubt remembering her own days in the classroom, waiting for the bell to ring to send her gleefully into biology class. "A little too much if you ask me."

"I think it was just that he was from Texas. She might have a thing for cowboys." Callie caught a glimpse of her sister's crumpled face before her professional smile slid into place. "Okay, maybe I'm grasping at straws. Especially if those stories of intimidation in the bathroom were true."

"So not going there." Cindy tipped her chin at the kids playing in the distance just as the bat cracked against the ball and sent it flying over left field. "She really can do it all, can't she?"

"Except math."

"What?" Cindy snapped her head around.

Callie's focus had returned to her team. "Deidra's a smart kid, but she's having a hard time getting her entrance exam scores high enough for the few colleges who are interested in her." Her gaze followed the star player who had made it safely to first base and was now inching her way towards second. She was planning to steal and the pitcher had yet to notice. "Excuse me."

Cindy nodded. "I need to be on my way to Mrs. Brogan's rabbit anyhow."

Her sister headed for the school building as Callie marched around the edge of the field till she stood behind the catcher. Her second best pitcher after Deidra stood poised to toss the ball when she noticed Callie barely tip her head toward first base.

By now Deidra had taken a suicide lead-off that had her nearly halfway between first and second. The girl had eyes like an eagle. Callie was pretty sure Deidra would spot her signals before the pitcher did. In a photo op worthy of a national sports channel close up, from the mound, the ball sailed through the air and arrived within the first baseman's grasp at the same second Deidra dove, hands first, safely back to first base.

Sure enough, the kid had spotted the play coming. It would be a darn shame if Deidra had to give up a scholarship opportunity over a few misplaced geometric angles and miscalculated statistics.

Callie had tapped every math teacher in the small high school for help. All had been willing but none had managed to instill enough understanding to up the athlete's ACT scores enough to make the grade.

The next slow pitch connected with the bat and the moment it skipped across the field, Deidra took off running for second. By the time the outfielder had the ball securely in glove, Deidra was rounding second and slid into third seconds before the ball made it to the baseman's glove. If that girl were a boy on the varsity baseball team, with her instincts for the sport, Callie would stake her lifetime savings and reputation that one day Deidra would be playing in the World Series. She let out a deep sigh. Of course, that would only be if they could find a way to fix the math. But how?

• • • •

A letter. Not even a full page letter. A note, really. Ten years, and no one at the top had the courtesy to sit Zane Crandall down in person to let him know his services were no longer needed. From the sudden blanket of near silence that had descended on the fifteenth floor, Zane guessed a couple dozen of his associates' services had proven expendable as well.

Rumors had been flying for weeks that the upcoming sale to some offshore conglomerate was going to cost a lot more jobs than the sunny speeches had implied. The same rumors had flown every time a shift in direction, or executives, had taken place in the past, and like the time before and the time before that, he and his comrades had weathered the storm, their jobs intact.

Today, that would not be the case. He stared at the stupid paper again. At least they'd offered an interesting severance package.

"You too?" Craig, his friend and cubicle neighbor, stood at the entry.

Zane nodded. "Any idea how many?"

"Too many." The lanky database specialist shrugged. "I seriously did not see this coming."

"I hear you." Zane leaned back in his seat and took a deep breath. Considering the chunk of change the company had spent for him to get his masters, he clearly had on rose colored glasses. The surprise was fading and his mind was now spinning with possibilities. "You know…"

His buddy crossed his ankles and leaned against the narrow wall.

"Maybe this isn't such a bad thing," Zane continued.

Craig straightened. "Said like a single man without children."

Zane raised a finger at his coworker. "No, hear me out."

"Okay." The man leaned against the wall again.

"How many of us have at one time or other talked about going out on our own? Doing things our way without input from the suits?"

"A lot." Craig chuckled. "I'd just like the idea better if it had come after my kids graduated high school, maybe college, and if there weren't so many of us out in the wilds of the unemployed all at the same time."

Zane knew exactly what Craig meant—at least the last part. With so many companies outsourcing anything and everything they could, short of the HVAC maintenance and janitorial, too many of them were going to be looking for work longer than they'd like. Plenty of others were about to find themselves foraging for a new career.

"You two commiserating or picking where to go for happy hour?" Another buddy came up. Over the next thirty minutes, Zane's oversized cubicle filled to capacity, reminding him of a packed can of sardines. Both those who'd been notified the upcoming changes were eliminating their jobs, and those who were informed they'd be doing more work indefinitely, were all chattering so fast and loud Zane was surprised the brass hadn't come down from the upper floors and tossed them all out on the spot.

According to his notice, he had seven days to wrap up his projects and hand them off. The thought made him dizzy. Especially since he liked the people who were getting dumped on to do their job and his. After hearing what the company had in mind, he was actually glad he was on the expendable list and not the still employed list.

"All right." Craig tapped his wedding ring on the wall's metal edging. "You joining us at the Social House or heading home?"

"I'm joining you." Who knew what kind of people he'd wind up working with next. He might as well enjoy what time he had left with folks he actually liked. "I just need to make one call and then I'll catch up with you all."

Craig nodded and headed down the hall. Zane could hear the voices fading in and out as folks closed down and made their way to the favorite after work watering hole.

Phone in hand, Zane tapped at the screen and waited for the familiar voice on the other end. "Hey Gramps."

Even though he'd been blessed to have four grandparents alive and well, Zane had always been closest to his mom's father. Most people were intimidated by the former military man, but once people got to know his grandfather, they discovered the loveable side that reminded Zane of the Pillsbury Doughboy.

"Well, isn't this a nice surprise this time of day." Zane could almost hear the frown descend on his grandfather's face. "Or is something wrong?"

"Depends on how you look at it. Some people might say things could be better."

"But…"

"But, the more I think about it, I believe things will be better."

"Better than what?" the old man groused.

"The company sale has eliminated my job." No point mentioning there were over thirty people in his department who had been eliminated with the brush of printer's ink. "So I've got some decisions to make."

His gramps cleared his throat. "You got options already?"

"More like ideas."

"When's your last day?"

"They've got me for seven more days, one hour, and," he flipped his wrist to look at his fancy computerized watch, "twelve minutes."

A bark of laughter bellowed through the air waves. He knew talking to his grandfather would lift his spirits. The man might be old, and occasionally gruff, but since retiring, he'd become optimistic and almost downright entertaining. "I have an idea. In a few weeks, I'm heading up to Lake Lawford to visit my old friend, the General. If something hasn't come up by then, why don't you join us?"

"At the lake?" Time with his grandfather didn't sound like a bad idea, but he wasn't so sure about a crusty old general.

"It's just lovely this time of year."

Zane considered his options. A few days at a peaceful lake with his grandfather, old general included or not, might be the perfect tonic for what ailed him. On the other hand, he had plenty of work to deal with right here in Boston.

"Best decisions are made with a clear head," his grandfather added, "and I can't think of a better place to clear your head."

There wasn't a single reason he could think of to say no to his grandfather. Besides, the man was probably right—a few days at the peaceful lake was just the sort of medicine the doctor would order. That is, if unemployment could be medicated.

Available at your favorite bookseller.

MEET CHRIS

USA TODAY Bestselling Author of more than a dozen contemporary novels, including the award-winning *Champagne Sisterhood*, Chris Keniston lives in suburban Dallas with her husband, two human children, and two canine children. Though she loves her puppies equally, she admits being especially attached to her German Shepherd rescue. After all, even dogs deserve a happily ever after.

More on Chris and her books can be found at
www.chriskeniston.com

Follow Chris on Facebook at ChrisKenistonAuthor
or on Twitter @ckenistonauthor

Questions? Comments?
I would love to hear from you.
You can reach me at chris@chriskeniston.com

* 9 7 8 1 9 4 2 5 6 1 4 6 0 *